*A
Harlequin
Romance*

OTHER
Harlequin Romances
by IRIS DANBURY

Many of these titles are available at your local bookseller, or through the Harlequin Reader Service.

For a free catalogue listing all available Harlequin Romances, send your name and address to:

HARLEQUIN READER SERVICE,
M.P.O. Box 707, Niagara Falls, N.Y. 14302
Canadian address: Stratford, Ontario, Canada.

or use order coupon at back of book.

A PAVEMENT
OF PEARL

by

IRIS DANBURY

HARLEQUIN BOOKS   TORONTO
WINNIPEG

Original hard cover edition published in 1974
by Mills & Boon Limited.

© Iris Danbury 1974

SBN 373-01873-8

Harlequin edition published May 1975

Printed in Canada

'We shall see, while above us
The waves roar and whirl,
A ceiling of amber,
A pavement of pearl.'

MATTHEW ARNOLD: *The Forsaken Merman*

CHAPTER ONE

RIANNA and her brother Martin walked along the wide street that bordered the quay. A row of dwarf palm trees stood at fairly regular intervals in front of a line of imposing hotels and blocks of flats.

"All the front rooms of these places have a marvellous view of the Mediterranean," remarked Rianna.

Martin was concentrating on finding the hotel, their rendez-vous for this morning's important appointment.

"Here it is," he said after a couple of minutes. "Hotel Bolzano."

A reception clerk told Martin that Mr. Holford Sinclair was out at the moment, but would return shortly.

"Then we'll have some coffee while we wait," replied Martin.

Half an hour later in the hotel lounge, Rianna glanced at her watch.

"Don't fidget," warned her brother.

"I suppose he really will turn up. We've come a long way if it's only on a fool's errand."

Martin laughed. "You *are* a pessimist," he rebuked her. "This is our big chance and you won't even give the man half an hour's grace!"

She relaxed and tried to concentrate on the possible outcome of this long, tedious wait. A month ago she had never imagined that yesterday she and Martin would be flying to Sicily and this morning they would be sitting in this hotel in Marsala, the sea-port town in the south-west corner of the island.

Rianna was not entirely happy about their prospective new venture. For the last three years she had helped her brother to make short films for educational authorities, travel companies and occasionally for television. In addition, Rianna wrote travel articles for newspapers and magazines, illustrating them with photographs taken either by herself or Martin. Together, the pair had covered many parts of the British Isles and a good deal of Europe, but when Martin heard of a chance of making an underwater film off the coast of Sicily, he was eager to seize the opportunity.

"You've not done much skin-diving," Rianna had objected when he first mentioned the idea.

"Enough to know how to avoid taking risks," he had assured her. "Besides, I want to know more about underwater cameras and this will give me the right experience."

"But where do I come in? I can swim quite well, but I'm no good at diving."

Martin had laughed then. "I told the agent I saw in London that my assistant and I had always worked together. He said he thought there'd be no difficulty about that with the leader of the expedition team. Besides, it's a wonderful chance for you to explore the island and write up dozens of articles — half a dozen books, even."

So on the strength of a vague promise, Rianna had accompanied her brother on what might turn out to be a wild-goose chase.

"If he turns you down, will he pay our travelling expenses, do you think?" Rianna asked now.

Martin was confident. "He won't turn us down. Experienced cameramen don't exactly grow on trees, and with you to help in the processing and clerical work —"

A tall slim man stood in front of Rianna.

"Mr. Derwent? I'm Holford Sinclair. Sorry to keep you waiting. I was delayed down at the harbour."

The glance he gave Rianna was questioning, as though he wondered what she was doing there beside Martin. His look was also disquieting.

"This is my sister Rianna," Martin introduced her.

Mr. Sinclair's face became blank. "You've come for a holiday, I take it?"

8

"Rianna is my assistant," Martin said quickly. "She does all the editing and clerical work."

Mr. Sinclair smiled faintly. "I'm afraid we can't take passengers aboard the yacht. We've no accommodation for – er – feminine members of the crew."

Martin opened his mouth to make some protest, but was then wise enough not to pursue the subject.

Mr. Sinclair began to discuss details of the work involved. "I think my agent in London probably explained that my regular cameraman has been injured in an accidental fire in the house where he was staying and he'll be out of action for some months. How much experience have you had of underwater camera work?"

Martin hesitated slightly. "Honestly, I'll admit not very much. A few dives off Cornwall and some in Scotland. But I think I can cope. You've received all the particulars of the films I've made up to date."

The two men continued their conversation and Rianna allowed her attention to focus on this man, Holford Sinclair, who might or might not employ one or both of the Derwent brother-and-sister team.

He was broad-shouldered, but as slim as one would expect a professional skin-diver to be. His features were pleasantly ordinary, dark hair, firm mouth and chin, but it was the incredible blueness of his eyes that caught the attention. Rianna judged him to be slightly under thirty and noted the small crinkles at the corners of his eyes. So he could laugh sometimes, she thought, although he was now addressing Martin in a very serious manner.

Suddenly he turned towards her and she flushed slightly as she realised he had caught her staring at him. "Our apologies, Miss Derwent, for neglecting you while we talked business. Let's go in to lunch, shall we?"

In the hotel restaurant, Rianna was aware of a certain tension in her brother. She had not particularly listened to every sentence of the discussion, but evidently matters had not gone too well and Martin's conversation was slightly forced and jerky.

9

She decided it was up to her to keep the ball rolling smoothly with Mr. Sinclair, if only for Martin's sake. He asked about her work as a travel journalist and seemed interested.

"If you haven't visited Sicily before, you should have plenty of scope," he assured her.

"That's what I told her," put in Martin eagerly.

"Then it will be something for you to do while the rest of us are grubbing about at the bottom of the sea."

She resented Mr. Sinclair's faintly patronising tone, as though she should occupy herself with knitting or embroidery while the men explored the sea-bed. "I try to concentrate on the lesser-known aspects of holiday travel," she said coolly, "the little odd corners and local customs that don't get into the travel agents' brochures."

When the meal was over and the three were taking coffee in the hotel lounge, Martin had relapsed into complete silence.

"Where are you staying?" Mr. Sinclair enquired, and Rianna told him the name of the hotel.

He nodded. "I can give you the addresses of several small, inexpensive hotels, if you're going to stay here for a lengthy period. You might find a small *pensione* very comfortable."

When the light caught his extremely blue eyes, Rianna was momentarily disconcerted. The eyes of a sailor, she told herself, or someone who was accustomed to focussing his gaze across vast land spaces.

When the three left the hotel, Mr. Sinclair called a taxi. "I'll take you down to the harbour where you can see the yacht," he suggested.

The *Celestina* rested gently at her mooring.

"She's not very large," commented Mr. Sinclair, "but adequate enough. Our quarters are a bit cramped, partly because the diving equipment takes up some of the space."

Rianna guessed that he was underlining the view he had expressed earlier – that there was no room aboard for a girl, even though she might be the sister of the cameraman. In any case, the graceful-looking yacht was smaller than she had imagined a ship equipped for diving would be and she could readily understand Mr. Sinclair's objections.

"I have to leave you now," he was saying to Martin. "I've several matters to attend to if we're going to start our next dive on schedule. I wonder if you and Miss Derwent would care to join me after dinner tonight at the Hotel Umberto. It's near the Cathedral. About nine-thirty or ten?"

"Yes, all right," agreed Marin.

Rianna watched Mr. Sinclair walk away, a strong, lithe figure who would not take kindly to opposition in his path.

"And what's the verdict?" she asked Martin.

He sighed and moved towards the harbour rail, clenching his hands on the top bar as he looked out across the blue satin sea.

"I'm not altogether sure," he admitted. "Apparently he'll take me on a month's trial and see how I shape, but as far as you're concerned, you already know that he won't have you aboard."

"Well, I didn't really expect to live on the ship all the time. Everything was so vague, and I've no idea how long these yacht trips last."

"I know, but I did think he'd allow you to do some of the work along with me, the film processing and writing up the details and records and all that."

"I could still help you with some of the work if I stayed ashore, but it makes it more difficult." Rianna linked her arm within Martin's. "Don't despair yet," she advised. "Perhaps when he sees that we work better together, he'll relent and let me come aboard at least sometimes."

Martin put his hand over hers. Then he grinned. "He seemed to think that perhaps you weren't really my sister and that I was trying to infiltrate his team by bringing along a girl-friend."

Rianna laughed. "What is he, then? A woman-hater? Evidently he can't bear his masculine world to be invaded by the opposite sex. He may be right. Perhaps he's afraid that my presence may turn the heads of all the rest of his crew and their work will go to pieces. Do reassure him that he need have no fears on that account."

Martin glanced at her face. "Oh, I don't know. You're not

11

as repulsive as that! I suppose if we looked more alike, he'd accept you, but with your hair –"

"It's not really red – only a reddish-brown," she protested. She knew it was true that although they shared a certain family resemblance, their colouring was quite different. Martin's fair hair and grey eyes were inherited fom his mother, whereas Rianna's dark copper hair and brown eyes had perhaps come from her father's sister, a ravishing auburn-haired beauty in her day.

"Why does he want to see us tonight?" Rianna asked Martin as they walked through the public gardens towards their hotel.

"I don't know. It's possible he might want me to meet other members of his team, but I don't know if they're already here yet."

Left to their own devices for the evening, Rianna would not have troubled to wear her newest evening dress, a cream jersey with bronze bead embroidery around the neck and a belt of dull gold plaques with vaguely Egyptian designs. But the fact that she was meeting Mr. Holford Sinclair again induced her to try to look her best, for Martin's sake. Even then, she was uncertain whether to appear reasonably smartly dressed or whether Martin's future would be assisted if she wore more workmanlike clothes on this particular occasion.

When she joined her brother in the lounge of the hotel where they were staying, he whistled and then grinned at her. "Well, naturally!" he teased. "If you're going to wear glamorous outfits like that, of course Holford Sinclair will be wary of you disrupting his ship."

"As long as I don't disrupt Mr. Sinclair, you've nothing to worry about," she retorted. "Anyway, it might be as well to let him see that I'm not going down on my knees begging him to let me come aboard to work with you. If he's a perverse type of man, he might easily swing the other way."

Martin nodded agreement. "As long as I'm not thrown out of the job because my dazzling sister has set out to fascinate the man."

Rianna grimaced at him. "And what likelihood is there of that? We don't know anything about him – whether he's married and has a brood of youngsters somewhere, along with a charming land-based wife."

After dinner, Rianna and Martin walked along the Via Scipione Africano towards the Hotel Umberto where they were to meet Mr. Sinclair again. Evidently this was one of the de luxe hotels of the town. The foyer glittered in a blaze of lights, the marble floors were tessellated in rich colours and the fragrance of flowers scented the air.

At the entrance to the hotel lounge Martin and Rianna stood for a moment or two surveying the crowded room until Holford Sinclair came hurrying towards them.

After greetings he conducted them to the far side to join half a dozen men and one woman. Introductions were made. "Miss Derwent and her brother, Martin. Allow me to present Signorina Emilia Cavallini."

Rianna was confronted by an exquisitely beautiful girl with satiny black hair, luminous smoke-grey eyes and a creamy complexion faintly flushed with pink like a delicately-tinted rose petal.

The other men were presented, two or three Italians, one Englishman, Duncan Merton, but Rianna was not sure if the latter were a member of Mr. Sinclair's diving team.

"Signor Medini is very important to our outfit," Mr. Sinclair was saying, and Rianna swiftly turned her face towards him. "He's the local man in authority for permission to make our diving expeditions. You understand that we must have a licence from the Italian Government before we can roam about as we choose in their coastal waters. So we have to pander to his wishes whenever possible." Mr. Sinclair smiled at the plump, bald-headed Italian opposite.

"Do not believe all he says." Signor Medini waved a plump, dismissing hand. "I am pestered every day by young men who seek treasure at the bottom of the sea."

"But we're not hunting for gold pieces," protested Mr. Sinclair. "Our interest is only in sea archaeology, the ships that were wrecked centuries ago and possibly the remains of buildings that were once on the land before the sea submerged them. Of

13

course," he added with a smile, "if we find bars of gold or a chest full of jewels, then it's some reward for our hard work."

The conversation continued in English and Italian, for Rianna noted that Emilia spoke perfect English, while Holford Sinclair was fluent in Italian. After a few minutes Rianna found that the young Englishman, Duncan Merton, had strategically changed places with Martin, and was now sitting beside her. This move ensured that Martin was now next to Emilia, with whom he seemed to be chatting non-stop.

"Is your brother joining our team?" asked Duncan now.

"We both hope so," Rianna replied, "but the decision rests with Mr. Sinclair. I think he's agreed to give Martin a month's trial."

"Good. Then you'll be staying here as well?"

"That depends," she answered cautiously. "If I can make good use of my time here, roaming about the island and filming some of the lesser-known sights, then I shall stay as long as Martin does."

In answer to his questions, she told him of the kind of work she did.

"When I've free time, I'd like to escort you to some of the places," he offered. "Sicily is a fascinating island, full of history, magic, surviving customs and wonderful colour."

"Thank you," she returned as non-committally as she could. "But probably your free time is limited. Are you one of Mr. Sinclair's team?"

"Yes. I'm his chief assistant, I suppose I could say. I've been associated with him on and off for about three years. I was with him in the Pacific a year or two back and also in the Gulf of Mexico and we've done a bit of work off Greece."

Rianna smiled. "Then you'll be able to give Martin some tips, as you're experienced."

"Of course. I'll do anything I can – for your sake," he added in an undertone. The expression on his tanned face caused Rianna to smile politely and then turn her head away. This young man was trying to forge ahead rather too fast for her liking and she had no intention of plunging into a reckless, and probably brief, romantic interlude with one of Martin's possible colleagues. As she looked away towards the other members of the party, her gaze was held by that of Holford Sinclair and momentarily she was disconcerted by that fixed stare. Was he weighing her up and pondering her usefulness or otherwise, even as a companion to her brother? He turned away quickly to speak to the man next to him and Rianna was relieved, although she could not define the reasons for that ease.

When eventually the party broke up shortly after midnight, Holford Sinclair evidently had a few more instructions for Martin, and Rianna waited while the two men finished their conversation. Signorina Emilia Cavallini was escorted to the hotel entrance by three men clustered around her and gave Rianna the merest farewell nod in passing.

In the homeward taxi, Martin was in buoyant spirits. "That girl Emilia – she's a stunner, isn't she?"

"She's very beautiful," admitted Rianna. "Almost too lovely to be true."

"Oh, she's true all right. Her father is one of the most important wine exporters here."

"Well, don't go overboard for her too soon. You never know whose toes you might be treading on," was Rianna's warning.

Martin flung back his head and laughed. "You do mix your metaphors, sweetie! It's almost impossible to tread on anyone's toes when you've dived overboard. Anyway, she was interested in you. Wanted to know if you were my girl-friend."

"Didn't she realise that we had the same surname?"

"Probably didn't listen. When I told her you were my sister, she gave me the most fascinating smile."

"Well, don't allow yourself to become too fascinated by her – or indeed any other girls here. After your recent experiences, it might be prudent to go slowly."

Martin grinned. "Yes, Grandmother. I might offer a word of advice to you on the same lines. I noticed that you were getting along fine with Duncan Merton."

Rianna laughed. "As far as I'm concerned, I was doing no more than making myself pleasant to the other members of your team. Did Mr. Sinclair say anything further about your working for him?"

"He wants me to have another medical examination here. I've shown him the certificates from London, but he said he'd like me to have a check-up from a local doctor, just to be on the safe side."

The next morning Rianna consulted her brother about a change of hotel. "I have these addresses from Mr. Sinclair. We could go and see the places and decide later when to make a move."

"You go and look at them," he suggested. "You're a better judge than I am. It's certainly true that we couldn't afford to live in this present hotel for any length of time. On the other hand, if Holford Sinclair turns me down after the month's trial, it seems hardly worth while moving about."

For a few moments Rianna was silent. Then she said, "Even if Mr. Sinclair did eventually turn you down as his cameraman, it might be a pity to throw away the chance of doing other work here in Sicily. The island is new to us and we could probably make some interesting films. Or I could go about on my own if you were busy diving for buried treasure."

Until that moment she had not thought clearly about the immediate future, taking the view that until Mr. Sinclair made his decision about Martin, all their plans were vague. Besides, only two days had elapsed since their arrival in Sicily. But now Rianna was eager to stay and work on her own if need be. Already she was drawn to this sun-drenched island with its flowers and the scented lemon groves, the temples and antiquities in the interior, and on the eastern side, the looming threat of snow-capped Mount Etna.

"And how do I get on if you're roaming about all over the place?" demanded Martin. "You're supposed to help me with the clerical work and keep a tab on my photos."

"I can still do that, even if Mr. Sinclair won't have women aboard the yacht. I'll go out and look at these hotels and see if any are suitable."

"See you at lunchtime, then," agreed Martin. "I'm meeting

Duncan Merton at the harbour." He gave his sister a teasing glance. "Come to think of it, perhaps he's the attraction. Yesterday you were convinced that we'd come here on a wild-goose chase. Now you're determined to stay here for most of the summer."

"Perhaps I'm a girl who's always prepared to make the best of disappointments," she retorted. There were two other comments she might have made, but she remained silent on those points. One was that she must convince Mr. Sinclair of her independence of spirit by occupying herself apart from the diving expedition.

The second matter was that Martin would doubtless enjoy further opportunities of developing his acquaintance with the beautiful Emilia. Just before last Christmas Martin's fiancée had suddenly broken off her engagement and within a month had married another man. The shock to Martin was considerable, for when she had returned his ring, he still had hopes of coaxing her into accepting it again, but that prospect was speedily extinguished when he heard news of her wedding.

"I can't believe it was all so sudden," he had remarked bitterly to Rianna at the time. "She was playing us off one against the other, so in the end it was a toss-up."

So now Rianna was not anxious for him to be involved in any kind of infatuation on the rebound. An English girl at home or here in Sicily might have been dangerous, but the lovely Emilia, daughter of prosperous wine-growers, and friend of Holford Sinclair, would be dynamite and fraught with all kinds of hazards for Martin.

The small hotels which Holford Sinclair had recommended were all clean and looked comfortable, but some distance from the harbour and perhaps not very convenient for her and Martin to work together, for the rooms were fairly small.

She tried the last address, a *pensione,* which was situated in a better position, but here again the rooms were small. Rianna made notes of the accommodation and the price and promised to let the proprietress know in a day or two what decision she and her brother would make.

17

"Signorina, there is something else," the woman began, and beckoned to Rianna to follow her. Rianna was not sure if she had correctly understood the Italian phrase, for as yet her knowledge of the language was hardly worth calling a smattering.

At the end of a passage, the woman opened a door leading to a small courtyard. Rianna followed her across the paved space and waited while the door of a single-storey building was unlocked.

"Signorina, please enter."

Rianna was charmed with this tiny villa, cottage or whatever one liked to call it. Three spacious rooms and a kitchen plus a bathroom which had apparently been added at a later date. She discussed the price and found that the terms for six months were very modest.

"I will tell my brother about it," she promised, "and we will come tomorrow together." The proprietress appeared to understand and Rianna wrote her name and the address of her present hotel on a scrap of paper.

When she saw Martin again at lunch, she was enthusiastic about her discovery. "It's just the place for us. I'm sure you'll find it comfortable and convenient. It's cheap, too. The woman says we can have any meals we want in the *pensione* itself, if we tell her perhaps an hour in advance. In any case, I found two small restaurants close by in the next street."

Martin smiled. "You seem to have decided already that we should take it. Is it furnished adequately?"

"Yes, furnished, but not too cluttered. Two bedrooms and a large sitting room. There's another thing – when we're both away, you on the yacht and perhaps I might be roaming about other parts of the island, we could leave our personal belongings there quite safely. Much better than leaving them in hotels."

It was not difficult next day to convince Martin of the suitability of the Casa Rosa, the pink house, and they paid a month's rent in advance, promising to move in a couple of days later.

A formal visit to the yacht, the *Celestina,* was fixed for this evening, Martin told her.

"Am I invited?" Rianna asked lightly. "Or warned off?"

18

"I've been requested to bring you."

"So that I can see for myself that the yacht is no fit place for women," she asserted.

She decided to wear a trouser suit with a frivolous nylon blouse. Mr. Sinclair would not be able to disapprove of her attire as unsuitable for clambering up and down companionways.

From the shore the yacht appeared fairly small, compared with others anchored close by, but Rianna noticed, as she had expected, that every square inch was used to the utmost.

Holford Sinclair explained that the vessel was on charter from the owner who was trying out a larger and more luxurious ship at present in Australian waters.

"Bigger and better yacht-progression," murmured Rianna. "Like changing your car each year for a newer and more expensive model."

Holford glanced at her with an amused expression. "You evidently don't approve of tycoons who own yachts, but we're very glad to have his second-best for a few months."

"And who sails the ship when all of you are busy pottering down below in the ocean?"

Holford laughed. "Naturally, the owner is prudent enough to put his own captain in charge or we might be tempted to make off with the yacht to some distant part of the world. Carlo is a retired naval officer and has a young man to act as mate, just a lad-of-all-work. In any emergency, a bad storm, for instance, all of us could help, of course. Does that satisfy your anxiety about the safety of the ship?"

She smiled and nodded. She had already been shown over part of the yacht and now Holford pointed out to her the captain's quarters, the men's cabins and the saloon where their meals were served, an apartment that had to do duty for a communal sitting room as well.

"Does Martin work in his own cabin?" she asked.

"If he wants to do so, yes. But he'll probably find it more convenient in this little cupboard of a place, where he has everything to hand."

Rianna inspected the "cupboard", where a swivel chair was

19

fixed to the floor and work benches, with shelves above, surrounded the occupant on three sides. A sliding door above a high storm step saved still more space.

"Very economical," she observed, realising that she was deliberately being shown the obvious impossibility of two people being able to work together in this congested space.

"We've found a tiny house to rent," she said later. "It's next door to the *pensione* you recommended. So if Martin wants to bring home some of his work, he'll be able to cope with it there."

"Oh, then you've beaten me to renting a villa. I'm still in the uncertain stage, but I don't care for living in hotels more than I need and I think I shall soon settle on one or another of those I've been offered."

When they reached the deck again, Duncan Merton came towards her with outstretched hand. "Nice to see you again, Rianna. How d'you like our nautical quarters?"

"I've been admiring the economy of space," she answered. "I can only hope that you all agree harmoniously all the time, no spare corners for sulking – or fights."

"We can't afford disagreements," cut in Holford Sinclair sharply. "That's why we have to make sure from the outset that we're all going to agree as a team."

"Of course," agreed Rianna, wondering if he had intended to rebuke her quite so smartly.

"By the way, we're all on Christian name terms here. May I call you Rianna? It's an unusual name."

"I think it's Welsh – or perhaps a corruption of a Celtic name, Mr. Sinclair."

Now he smiled and his piercing blue eyes lost a little of their frosty character. "Holford – I hope?"

She nodded with a smile and thought that perhaps that was one more small hurdle overcome in the matter of this somewhat thorny relationship with her brother's employer – or possible employer.

Martin had not yet heard the complete results of the new medical test he had taken at Holford's request, so nothing could be decided for certain yet.

Rianna had not realised that she and Martin and the others were expected to dine aboard the yacht tonight, but she was delighted to view the deepening sunset sky across the violet sea to the west and the group of Egadi Islands tinted with a lavender light. Landwards, the town of Marsala, stretching in several directions on Sicily's most westerly point, became pinpointed with lights springing up like fireflies and even as Rianna watched, twilight veiled the tall modern buildings, the church domes and steeples, the clusters of red-roofed houses.

Below in the saloon Rianna was surprised at the extent and variety of the dishes served. Tunny fish with a piquant sauce was followed by small medallions of pork sprinkled with red peppers. She was offered a choice of various cheeses or a sweet which looked like cheesecake, but was flavoured with pine-nut.

"Or of course you can have both," suggested Holford.

She chose the sweet and found it delicious. Apparently Jeffrey, who had been introduced to her as the marine biologist of the team, was also the cook.

"He's more or less our resident chef," explained Holford. "At first we used to take it in turns to cook the meals, but that turned out to be a haphazard affair, ranging from almost uneatable stew to some choice burnt offerings. Now, Jeffrey copes most of the time single-handed and in his own way."

"I shall have to take a few lessons from you," Rianna suggested with a smile at the young man who was slightly embarrassed by these unexpected compliments. "I realise how difficult it must be to manage in so small a space as your tiny galley."

"You just have to devise your own methods," answered Jeffrey.

On deck again, the yacht seemed encircled by velvety blackness, except on the landward side where the lights of the city blazed like a handful of jewellery.

Duncan Merton drew a chair closer to Rianna's against the awning which acted as a windbreak. "Will you be cold out here?" he asked solicitously.

"No. I find it pleasant to be able to sit about in the open on a March evening," she answered.

"I wish we could find it as pleasant and comfortable in the water, but as you probably know, the sea temperature takes longer to warm up than the land."

"But it also retains the heat in the autumn, so you can continue diving in warmer water than the land temperature."

Duncan smiled. "Have you done any skin-diving?"

"No, and I'm not very keen to try. I can swim and dive from a small boat or raft, but that's about the extent of my water prowess. Martin is the expert, although of course he lacks the experience of you and Holford – Mr. Sinclair – and the others."

"He'll speedily learn," prophesied Duncan. After a pause, he added, "If you change your mind and want to explore the depths, I'd be very pleased to teach you."

"And what lessons are you proposing to give Rianna?" queried a voice at Rianna's side. Holford's figure had loomed out of the shadowy darkness.

"Only tuition in skin-diving," answered Duncan, and Rianna immediately detected a sarcastic edge to his voice.

"And are you enthusiastic about learning?" Holford asked her.

"Not particularly, but in due course I might be overcome by a desire to discover the secrets of the sea." She spoke lightly, thinking that this was possibly the best way to deflect Duncan's offer of help. But Holford said almost savagely, "Never under-estimate the power of the sea. There are plenty of mysteries yet that we don't understand – perhaps never will."

She was immediately routed by this rebuff and was on the point of making the excuse that she felt cold and would seek shelter below, when Duncan muttered, "See you later, perhaps, Rianna," and melted away in the shadows. Holford immediately took the vacant chair.

She hardly knew whether to be glad or sorry at this substitution. Yet at all costs, she must avoid antagonising Holford, even if she was not disposed to cringe or fawn upon him, for the sake of Martin.

"I probably spoke thoughtlessly about the sea," she admitted, aware that the awkward silence must be broken. "I'm not really venturesome."

He shifted slightly in his chair and although she could not see the expression in his eyes, his nearness had a disturbing effect upon her, one that she could not really account for.

"I've had the doctor's report on Martin," he said abruptly, ignoring her half-apology. "It seems quite satisfactory, but of course you understand that there's more to our kind of job than physical fitness."

"Naturally." She wondered whether these remarks were leading up to a refusal to take Martin and he was employing this method of softening the blow.

"I think your brother has the right kind of temperament, but we shall do a few practice dives together and we can both find out."

"Thank you. It will mean a lot to Martin if you really accept him. I mean after the month's trial."

"Do you suppose he's really dedicated to underwater study? Or is it just a new field, an added experience of a different kind of photography?"

"I don't think you can ask me that," she told him a trifle bluntly. "I doubt whether even Martin could answer satisfactorily at this stage."

She heard his quiet laugh. "That was well said. One of Martin's chief assets is the loyalty of his sister."

There was nothing she could say in reply to this unexpected compliment. Adroitly, he changed the subject and asked about her family.

"I'm not being merely inquisitive, I hope," he said hastily. "It helps me to understand my team better if I know even vaguely something of their home circumstances."

"Yes, I can see that," she answered readily. After a slight pause, she began. "Our mother died nearly ten years ago when Martin was fourteen and I was nearly thirteen. A cousin of my father's came to live with us for a time, but when she left after about a year, we found we could manage quite well by ourselves. I think she upset my father more than she did us. He's a lecturer at a local college and likes his quiet routine, his books, and hates being tidied up."

"What is his subject?" Holford enquired.

"History. But he's also very addicted to mathematics and occasionally takes a student or two for coaching for their exams." Rianna laughed quietly. "He says he enjoys two different worlds of study. History is unpredictable and mathematics is predictable up to a point."

"How does he claim that history is so unpredictable if the events have already happened?"

"Oh, he says you can find a hundred instances for speculation – if Napoleon had done this instead of that, if someone hadn't died conveniently and left a throne vacant for a contender – if someone had opposed instead of yielding. My father can find dozens of incidents that have changed the course of history.

"Yes, I see what you mean," murmured Holford.

"We found my father great fun during the holidays," continued Rianna. "Walking tours and camping and he encouraged us in all kinds of hobbies – nature study, painting. I realise now that he was trying to teach us to *see,* not just give things a passing glance. He bought Martin his first simple camera and suggested he should do his own developing and printing instead of sending the snaps to the local chemist. We went to churches and ancient buildings and he taught us about different styles of architecture. He always had *time* for us when we were young."

"And now? How does he manage without either of you?"

"He has a daily housekeeper. Our home is near St. Albans and he's happy to see us between our spells of work and travel. If possible, we try to make our breaks coincide with his holidays."

"But that won't happen this time until perhaps the late summer? If Martin can stand the pace, we shall be very busy right up to the end of September. Or do you plan to go home earlier?"

"Does that mean you regard me as a hindrance?" she challenged in her smoothest voice.

"Not in the least," he answered, but there was a tiny pause before he had spoken, as though he were unsure.

"I shall make my plans as I go along," she went on. "As you pointed out, there's plenty on the whole island of Sicily to occupy me for several months."

In the darkness she thought that last remark of hers should satisfy him that she was not to be sent packing because he could not avoid splitting up the brother-and-sister team.

He rose abruptly. "I'm afraid I've kept you up here too long and let you get cold. I'm sorry."

During the conversation with him, she had not noticed whether she was chilly, but she realised that the excuse was valid enough for an end to a quiet talk. He certainly knew how to dismiss a girl when the moment suited him.

Martin came along the deck. "Perhaps it's time we went ashore," he suggested. "Ready, Rianna?"

"Quite ready," she answered, not wanting to outstay her welcome, yet desirous of cherishing in her memory this night aboard the *Celestina*, as the sole woman in the company of the men, for it was uncertain when she would again be invited, or if at all.

Duncan steered the small motor-dinghy across the short distance to the harbour wall and helped Rianna up the stone steps. Martin was talking to Jeffrey who had also come ashore.

"There's something you ought to know," Duncan said to Rianna in a quiet voice as he walked along with her.

"Don't let me be a party to anyone's guilty secret," she said flippantly.

"This is different. Holford needs to be extremely fussy over selecting any new member of the team. That's why he's giving your brother such a stiff test, and when we actually go diving, Martin will have to face even stiffer trials. The fact is — we lost a man last year in the Pacific."

"You mean he died? He was drowned?"

"Yes. He seemed fit enough — but he didn't surface at the right time — and he was dead when we pulled him on board. The trouble is that Holford blames himself for the accident. The man was married and left a young wife, so Holford feels he's responsible."

"But if it was an accident?"

"Naturally it was an accident. We don't fight each other down below — too dangerous."

By now Martin was close behind Rianna and Duncan.

"Don't let Martin know about this. He'll probably hear about it later on, but not now –"

"Why shouldn't he know?" demanded Rianna in an undertone. "The man was one of our cameramen."

There was no time for further explanation, as Martin had caught up, apologising for delay. "I was just talking to Jeffrey."

When Rianna and Martin had arrived at their hotel, she was wondering why Duncan had thought fit to tell her this past episode. Was he trying to show Holford in a bad light? A leader who disregarded the absolute safety of his team? Or was he trying to discourage Martin from joining the team? She thought this seemed unlikely, for if Martin decided not to accept Holford's offer, he and Rianna would undoubtedly return to England, even if they stayed a few weeks together filming the island.

On first acquaintance Duncan had appeared rather more than eager for Rianna to stay quite a long time in Sicily. Not that she was particularly drawn to him. In her room, after she had said goodnight to her brother, Rianna fiercely told herself that she was not drawn to any of the men she had so far met in the team. She had work to do and no time for dallying with any of them, least of all Holford. That last thought made her smile, as she brushed her dark copper hair in front of the mirror. Much more likely that Holford would never have time for dallying with her. Probably he could not help the fact that his blue-eyed gaze had a disturbing effect on women, so there was no need for her to take a few glances seriously. Next time she met him she would focus her attention on his chin or his tie, if he were wearing one, and avoid staring him straight in the eye.

CHAPTER TWO

DURING the next few days while Martin was occupied in daily swimming exercises and diving tests, Rianna began the task of moving in to the Casa Rosa and arranging her own and her brother's possessions.

"I didn't bring much of my own gear with me," Martin had remarked, "because I assumed most of the equipment would be on board the yacht."

"And so it is," agreed Rianna. "What you need here at home are probably a few notebooks, a card index, a few odds and ends which we can easily buy here in the town."

She had of course brought her portable typewriter, together with the ciné camera and two other cameras, with a supply of the correct films. She knew from experience that if she intended to film out-of-the-way spots, she must always carry her own supplies, for small villages might not stock the exact sizes or kinds.

She found a suitable table in one of the bedrooms and transferred it to the living room. Signora Offredi, who kept the *pensione* adjacent, was helpful and supplied several more chairs and a cupboard in which Rianna could keep her manuscripts and Martin's reports and records.

Then Rianna applied her efforts to the kitchen, but the curious contraption that seemed to be a stove alarmed her. "How on earth does the thing work?" she muttered, but Signora Offredi came to the rescue, not only instructing Rianna as to its vagaries, but also unearthing a small electric cooker in a cardboard box.

"That's better," said Rianna thankfully. "I shall manage much better on that." They were confident words, for the first morning that Martin and she breakfasted together, she managed to burn the toast, while the coffee remained half cold.

"No doubt I shall learn in time," she commented philosophically. "In the meantime, we'd better stick to rolls and peach jam and I'll concentrate on making the coffee really hot. This cooker isn't geared to English breakfasts of eggs and bacon."

"Just as well, perhaps," Martin laughed. "I have to watch my slender waistline."

"Well, Holford could hardly find fault with your figure," Rianna returned. "Not an ounce of extra fat on you."

"Still, he never fails to warn me each day that fat is the enemy of divers. By the way, he plans to sail the yacht over to one of the Egadi islands later this week. He says the dives are more difficult there than here in Marsala and it will be good practice for me."

Rianna glanced apprehensively at her brother. "I hope he's not going to be too severe in putting you through your paces."

"No, I think I shall be able to manage. He has excellent maps on which every little bit of coast is marked not only with the depth of water, but there are signs belonging to a code that shows how difficult they are. Some mean that anyone who can use a snorkel can play about, but others need proper scuba apparatus."

Rianna knew that the word "scuba" meant the self-contained underwater breathing apparatus that was possibly the one item most responsible for modern interest in exploring the sea.

"Will Holford accompany you on these dives?" she now asked.

"Naturally. He's the headmaster and wants to see for himself how I cope."

"So you'll probably be away for a few days?"

"I don't know. He'll probably give us some idea of the date when we'll be back. What will you do with yourself in the meantime?"

"Well, while I'm in Marsala, I thought I'd try to find out something about the wine trade here, link it perhaps with some of the history of the town and photograph some of the interesting odd corners."

"Emilia's father could give you all the information you want

28

about the wine-growing and exporting. Pity I can't accompany you all the time. I'd like to see Emilia again."

Rianna gave her brother a glance of amusement. "No doubt she's reserved for some noble and wealthy Italian, a marriage to unite two patrician families. You'd better be careful."

"We'll see what else in the way of feminine attraction the island has to offer. It's early days yet."

In one way she was glad to find that Martin was trying to recover his good spirits after the crushing disappointment he had experienced only three months ago, when his fiancée had deserted him.

As long as he did not strike up a too impetuous infatuation with any one girl during the summer, she judged that there might be safety in numbers.

When Martin had gone to his morning swimming exercises, she idled for a while about the little Casa Rosa, fidgeting with an ornament here, a chair there, her mind far away from her immediate surroundings. She wondered if she would meet any of the diving team again before the trip to the Egadi islands. Left on land, she began to feel like a sailor's wife when the men have put to sea.

Then she smiled at her absurd thoughts and switched her mind to something more practical. The best way to introduce herself to the wine-growing firm of Cavallini, perhaps. She also needed maps of the island and street plans of some of the towns.

She spent the morning in the shopping streets where she made the necessary purchases and added several guide-books to her collection. She looked for a restaurant for lunch and found one near the Cathedral. At an outside table, she practiced her few words of Italian on the waiter, who smilingly corrected her pronunciation, then hurried away to bring her order.

Studying the phrase book later when her coffee was served, she did not hear a greeting close by. When she recognised the English voices, she saw Duncan and Holford by her table.

"I've bought a simple phrase-book," she explained. "I thought a little basic Italian might be an advantage, but it has the oddest sentences in it – like this one – 'An old ox draws a straight furrow.' Now I wonder in what circumstances I might be able to use that."

The two men sat down, one on each side of her and bent their heads towards the book. Duncan turned a page. "Here's a choice one –' 'A woman and glass are always in danger.'"

Holford laughed. "In danger? Doesn't it mean they are dangerous?"

"Your Italian is better than mine." Duncan pushed the book across. "I've noticed that the fishes don't speak Italian when we meet them in the ocean, so it's no use our asking the way."

Holford's head was bent close to Rianna's. " 'Greed chokes the puppy,' " he read, then laughed again. "I can probably lend you several little books that might suit your purpose better. Simple questions and not so many proverbs."

"Yes, I need to know first – how much or how do I find the way to such-and-such a place?"

Duncan signalled to a waiter to bring coffee and unaccountably Rianna was pleased to have the company of these two men even for a quarter of an hour or so.

"Have you made any plans yet for your trips into the deep interior of the island?" Holford asked her.

"Not yet. I thought while you were away at the islands – Martin told me that you intend to go over to the Egadis –" Then she broke off, feeling that Holford might have some reason for not wanting her to discuss his plans, but he merely nodded, and she continued, "So I thought I'd find my way about Marsala itself. It looks such an interesting town. Also, I'd like to know something about the wine industry here. Would it be possible to get in touch with the firm of Cavallini?"

"Easily," replied Holford. "I can take you there myself this afternoon if that's convenient."

"Thank you, that would help, although I don't want to take up your time."

She happened to glance swiftly at Duncan and noticed an amused smile playing around his mouth, although his eyes were downcast and she could not see their expression.

After a few moments, Duncan rose. "If you're going to escort

Rianna to the Cavallini wine-cellars, I'll be off," he said to Holford. "No chance of seeing the beautiful Emilia there, I suppose?"

"She's no career girl," answered Holford, "and certainly not her father's right hand."

Rianna caught the faintly acid tone in Holford's voice, but he smiled at Duncan, who waved goodbye and walked away from the café.

"Do you feel equal to walking or shall we take a taxi?" suggested Holford, after a long pause following Duncan's departure. "It's not really far."

"I'll walk," she decided briskly. "Later on, in the summer, I shall be glad of an afternoon siesta, but the weather's not too hot now."

On the way he pointed out various little alleys where interesting buildings were tucked away, showed her the doorway of what had once been a palatial mansion and now housed a dress factory.

Signor Cavallini welcomed Holford and Rianna to his office, offered glasses of Marsala and agreed without hesitation to have Rianna conducted over his wine-making establishment.

"Perhaps a morning?" he suggested. "Then you will have ample time for your notes." He seemed delighted with the idea of articles being written about his firm.

Rianna modestly pointed out that she had no commissions from editors, but only hoped to sell her material to likely magazines.

"I'm sure you need have no fear that Miss Derwent's efforts will be in vain," put in Holford, to Rianna's surprise. "She's most competent and doesn't undertake projects that she can't carry out successfully."

Rianna shot him a glance of thanks. Discussions took place as to the most suitable day, the available photographs that could be provided by the publicity department and other details that would save Rianna endless notes.

When she accompanied Holford out into the street again, she said, "That was a leap in the dark you took on my behalf. How

31

do you know that I won't botch the visit?"

He paused in the middle of the pavement and although she had advanced a pace or two, she was forced to turn back to look at him. "You don't look like a botcher to me," he said gravely.

They resumed walking, but she now kept her gaze fixed on the scene ahead, the tall buildings either side of the dark blue sea. "Thank you," she murmured after a moment. "I must try to live up to your lofty notions about me." Only by treating the matter lightly could she keep control of the warm delight she felt in this man's presence and, even more, in his expressed faith in her capacity for competent work.

"I'd like to see your little villa, if I may," he suggested. "If Martin is planning to do some of his work there, I'd like to make sure he's comfortable. There might be some of our equipment on board which we could well spare and send it to your place."

"Yes, of course," she said hurriedly, mentally surveying the Casa Rosa as to its state of tidiness to receive visitors.

He hailed a taxi and she gave the driver the address. Signora Offredi, the owner of the *pensione*, had given Rianna a key to a door in the street wall, so that she did not always have to go through the *pensione* itself.

Holford expressed his pleasure at so neat a little house. "You've done well to find this so easily. When I gave you the name of the *pensione*, I had no idea this little property was attached."

"I think I can make it comfortable for us both," she returned, then flushed at the word "us". "For Martin and me, I mean. I shall buy a few extra pieces of furniture – a couple of chairs and a small table that we can use in the courtyard, one or two pots and pans for cooking and so on."

Holford seemed in no hurry to leave and she was reluctant to suggest that he might have other demands on his time. He might assume that she was anxious for his departure, and the truth was far different. She enjoyed his company and hoped that his present genial mood would endure. Martin's future was dependent on Holford's goodwill and Rianna told herself that she must do nothing to disturb amicable relations.

She made some coffee and apologised for the fact that she had neither biscuits nor little cakes to offer him. "I haven't yet begun to cater for anything except our breakfast," she said. "We've taken some of our meals in the *pensione* so far. I'm afraid I have to learn my way about the cooking equipment here."

"If you're in a difficulty, you must let Jeffrey know. He seems to be able to cook on any kind of contraption. Must have been a boy scout."

When eventually Holford rose to leave, he gazed around the sitting room. "Yes, not bad at all. Much better than trying to live in hotels."

As he crossed the courtyard, Martin came in through the passage from the *pensione*. The two men greeted each other then walked across the courtyard with Martin doing the talking and Holford listening, with an occasional nod.

Rianna remained in the doorway of the Casa Rosa, aware that they might be discussing business details. Then at the gate in the wall, Holford turned to smile at Rianna and waved a goodbye. Unaccountably, she experienced a tremor of pleasure and turned away swiftly to go inside the house. She felt the flush rising into her cheeks and was annoyed with herself for behaving like a very adolescent schoolgirl.

"Holford been here long?" queried Martin as he came indoors.

"He took me to see Signor Cavallini and arrange for a visit to the cellars and vaults and so on. Then we came back here. He wanted to see our little shack."

Martin smiled and nodded. "I see. He wants to keep tabs on me and make sure that I'm not living next to a cabaret place or notorious night-club."

Rianna let that remark go. That view had not occurred to her. In her enthusiasm for Holford's company, she had imagined that he was interested in the temporary home which she would share with her brother.

"When are you going to the islands?" she asked, changing the subject.

"In about two or three days' time. Friday, I think, he wants to leave."

"Friday? Surely no sailor ever wants to set out on a Friday!"

Martin grinned. "Holford doesn't go by sailors' rules."

Or anyone else's, thought Rianna. She guessed that to him the most important rules were those of the sea – and his own.

Two days later Riana was surprised by a visit from Jeffrey, the biologist of Holford's team.

"Holford said you weren't very happy with your cooking facilities here," he said. "Mind if I have a look?"

"Go ahead by all means." She invited him in, but he hesitated. "There's a van outside with some pieces of furniture to deliver. Will you show the man where to put them?"

"Furniture?" echoed Rianna. But already Signora Offredi was out in the courtyard with a man following. He was carrying several chairs stacked one on the other.

Bewildered, Rianna instructed the man to leave them in the shady corner of the courtyard. Four chairs, a round table and two folding chairs. She signed the receipt and was aware of Signora Offredi's beaming approval.

"Very good," said the Italian woman. "You will be able to sit out here and eat or work – or even sleep," she added with a chuckle.

"Yes. Oh, yes," returned Rianna absent-mindedly. These items could have been sent only by Holford – unless of course Martin had ordered them. She decided not to express her ignorance to Jeffrey who was poking about in the kitchen, muttering a blend of imprecations and advice to sundry pieces of metal which he had strewn on a newspaper on the floor.

"Now let's see if it fits together," he murmured after a while. "Either it will function or blow us up."

"In that case, I shall retreat before you set a match to it," Rianna warned him, and promptly took herself out into the courtyard. After a few seconds, he called, "O.K.!" and she re-entered the kitchen to find Jeffrey triumphantly surveying the stove now burning with a steady yellow flame.

"The affair needs a good clean-up," he remarked, "but even so, it will work tolerably well, on the right kind of oil. No doubt your Signora here will be able to supply that."

"Thank you very much," murmured Rianna, who still had reservations about using such an unfamiliar kind of stove.

As he washed the dirt and grease off his hands, he queried, "Furniture all right?"

"Oh yes. Just what I wanted. Chairs and a table that we can use indoors or outside."

"Holford knows his way about. Speaks Italian better than any of the rest of us and is first-rate at bargaining. You were right to let him attend to the buying."

Rianna smiled and nodded. Of course that was the line she must take, that Holford had acted as her purchasing agent. She was grateful to Jeffrey for showing her how to deal with this unexpected situation. Evidently he knew that Holford had instructed the shop what to deliver.

"Will you stay and have lunch with me?" she invited. "Pot luck, I'm afraid, because – er –"

"Because I've been fiddling about here, naturally. No, thanks all the same, but I can take you to a nearby *trattoria* which I know. That is, if you care to come."

"I'd like to. It's always useful to know which places a woman can enter without twenty men looking up from their plates as if a creature from Mars had suddenly blown in."

Jeffrey laughed. "Wrong planet. Should be Venus." Then he grinned. "No, I've remembered. They're supposed to be green or blue or something of the sort. Shall we go?"

In the *trattoria* with its red-checked tablecloths, plain wooden chairs, and advertisements for various wines the chief wall decorations, Rianna noticed that Jeffrey was not the rather shy young man she had first met on board the yacht. He chatted about his training as a biologist, his decision to specialise in the marine side of the work and his enthusiasm for the underwater world.

"In some places it's like a world of jewels," he told her. "Sea-anemones the colour and shape of tomatoes and grottoes that look as though they're padded with blue and green velvet. People who don't dive don't know what they're missing."

She reflected that Holford seemed to be fairly lucky in his selection of his team and she hoped that her brother's enthusi-

35

asm for underwater work would earn him Holford's lasting approval.

After leaving Jeffrey, who said that later in the afternoon he had to fulfil his swimming and other keep-fit exercise programme, Rianna strolled towards the main shopping streets.

In one way she felt that she was idling away time that ought to be spent in collecting material for illustrated articles, but no date had yet been fixed for her visit to the Cavallini establishment and until then she did not want to travel far out of Marsala.

When she arrived back at the Casa Rosa, Signora Offredi gave her a telephone message.

"Signor Sinclair?" echoed Rianna. "Yes? What message?"

"He said to go to the Hotel Bolzano as soon as you can."

"Bolzano. That's the hotel where he's staying." Her thoughts flew to Martin and she almost panicked. Had some disaster happened to her brother?

"Perhaps I could use your telephone, *signora*, and speak to Signor Sinclair?"

In the small entrance hall of the *pensione*, Rianna leaned against the wall in relief at hearing Holford's voice.

"Yes. No, it's nothing to do with Martin," he had answered crisply in reply to her immediate query. "It's a – a personal matter – I think you might be able to help me."

In her relief at Martin's safety, she forgot to be surprised that he should ask for her help.

"I'll get a taxi and come at once," she promised. She left a message for Martin in case he should arrive home and wonder where she was.

At the Hotel Bonzano she waited only a few minutes in the lounge before Holford came down in the lift.

"I've an unexpected visitor," he began. "Mrs. Patterson has arrived for a holiday. She's the wife – well, her husband was one of my team some time ago. She's not in very good health – and very tired after the journey – well, you'll see for yourself."

Rianna, mystified, accompanied him to a room on the second floor. There was no occupant, but Holford motioned her towards the open french windows. On the balcony in the shade, resting on a chaise-longue was a young woman, fair-haired, pale-faced and evidently very weary.

"Lynda, this is Miss Derwent," Holford introduced. "Rianna, Mrs. Patterson."

Mrs. Patterson half smiled in acknowledgment. Holford bent over her to ask, "How do you feel now?"

"Oh, so very tired." She looked up at Holford with an expression that Rianna did not quite know how to interpret. Adoring? Or just the aftermath of fatigue?

Holford patted the young woman's hand and she curled her fingers around his. "You must rest as much as you can," he advised. "You really shouldn't have come here so soon after your illness," he added, but there was only the mildest rebuke in his tone.

"I simply couldn't endure staying in England any longer. It's been such a long winter. I longed for the sun." Mrs. Patterson smiled at Holford. "And you said I could come here at any time."

"Yes, of course," he answered quickly. Too quickly, thought Rianna. "You should be able to get well here in a good climate, and – Rianna will help you all she can."

"Thank you," murmured Mrs. Patterson.

Holford drew Rianna into the bedroom. "Mrs. Patterson has recently been ill. I don't feel that I can leave her alone in a hotel like this. As you know, we're planning to go over to the islands tomorrow – and apart from that, there'll be times when we're away for several days at a time."

"What do you want me to do?" asked Rianna crisply, feeling that this was the best way of helping him to cut his explanations short.

"The villa I'm trying to rent isn't quite ready yet, so I wondered if you could have Lynda – Mrs. Patterson, to stay with you for the few days we shall be away. Martin won't be there, so you'd have a room."

"But does she need nursing or medical attention?"

"Oh, no, not at all. She's just fagged out at the moment. If I'd

37

known she intended coming just now I'd have made other arrangements for her, but she arrived without warning."

"What are you plotting, you two?" came Mrs. Patterson's voice from the balcony.

"Trying to settle what is best for you," returned Holford, raising his voice slightly. Then he added in an undertone, "Could you help me, Rianna?"

"Of course," she answered at once, not pausing to think of any ultimate outcome, but only of the opportunity to be of service to Holford. "I'll do my best to see that she's comfortable."

His smile was reward enough and as he grasped her hand, she experienced again that quiver of delight at his touch.

He returned to the balcony. "Rianna will look after you for a few days while we're over at the islands," he assured Mrs. Patterson.

"But why can't I stay here?"

"It's a comfortable hotel, of course, but you'll be better staying with Rianna. She has a most engaging little villa."

Rianna now joined him on the balcony. "Have you a special diet, Mrs. Patterson?"

"Do call me Lynda. No, nothing special. I eat so little."

"Probably that's half your trouble," said Holford, "so we must cure that. How do you feel about having dinner with me?"

Rianna noticed the instant animation on Lynda Patterson's features. "Down in the restaurant? Oh, I think I'd like that."

"Well, I was going to suggest up here, but if you prefer the restaurant – Rianna, you'll join us, won't you?"

Lynda's eyes closed. "Perhaps it would be better up here after all," she murmured weakly.

"Oh, no, I insist," protested Holford. "It would do you more good to be among a few people instead of moping up here."

"Moping?" she echoed in a gentle voice. "Oh, no, not that."

Rianna turned away, a wave of despondency in her heart. "I think I'd better not stay," she said quietly to Holford.

"Oh, but you must. I've a lot to talk about and I shan't have time to-morrow. Martin can fend for himself, can't he?"

"Yes, he'll get a meal in a restaurant or at the *pensione* where we live."

"That's settled, then." Holford's face which had been worried a few minutes ago began to look more relaxed and cheerful. "I'll leave you both now for half an hour or so. Probably Lynda might like help in changing her dress."

So as well as nurse, she was to be lady's maid now, thought Rianna rebelliously, but she adopted an amiable manner towards this fragile girl who seemed to have some extraordinary power to exert over Holford.

When Lynda chose a turquoise evening dress with elaborate pearl embroidery on the bodice, Rianna felt out of place and rather too workmanlike in her trouser suit of sea-green crimplene with a cream shirt.

"Such an effort to dress up," murmured Lynda. "It would have been better to have stayed up here, I think."

Rianna did not reply, although she agreed, but she began to suspect that Lynda would have preferred a tête-à-tête dinner with Holford almost anywhere, rather than the intrusion of another girl.

When the lift reached the ground floor, Lynda tottered shakily across the intervening space towards Holford and almost fell into his arms. Rianna felt guiltily that she had neglected her charge already, although Lynda had been eager to step out of the lift the moment she saw Holford standing there.

There was another surprise for Rianna. Duncan Merton joined Holford in the lounge and greeted Lynda with all the ease of a former acquaintanceship.

"Good to see you," he said to Lynda, "although I'm sorry you've been ill. Better now?"

"Improving," she answered with a radiant smile.

During the meal Lynda maintained a gay, bantering conversation with the two men, talking of people and incidents known to all three, but leaving Rianna out on the fringe. This meeting seemed to be in the nature of a reunion and was full of "Do you remember?" Rianna pinned a smile firmly to her lips, ate the various dishes presented and sipped only a moderate quantity

39

of wine, in contrast to Lynda who had her glass refilled several times.

Rianna had the chance to study this girl who had, as it were, pitchforked herself into the tight circle of Holford and his team. Her fair hair was shoulder-length and gleamed like silk under the chandeliers. Dainty features and a well-formed chin, an almost waxen pallor now relieved by two rather hectic spots of colour on her cheeks; Lynda possessed that slight, delicate build that induced men to want to protect her, to wrap her in warm protection and swathe her in the softest luxury. Yet it was Lynda's eyes that seemed to Rianna to reveal a nature quite contrary of fragility. They were blue-grey but reflected a hardness hidden often behind fluttering lashes. Holford's eyes held a piercing blue quality, but on most occasions they sparkled with amusement or interest.

"And what are you doing with yourself when we've all gone off to the Egadis?" Duncan's voice close to her ear recalled Rianna to the present situation.

"Oh, I've plenty to occupy me," she answered with a smile, thinking of the extra task that Holford had given her in looking after a semi-invalid who tonight appeared in excellent health. "I shall start preparing my itineraries for trips around the island, so that when Martin is away with the rest of you, I can do my own work straightaway."

"What is your own work?" asked Lynda.

"Rianna is a most successful writer," Holford answered immediately.

Lynda's finely arched eyebrows rose questioningly. "You write books? Fiction?"

"Oh, no. Fact is my line. Articles, travel, customs and so on. Usually illustrated." Then Rianna added firmly, "I take photographs or films – or use my brother's." That should forestall any such phrase from Lynda as – "Oh, you sketch or paint."

"I'm afraid I'm quite a useless creature," wailed Lynda now that she had the attention of both men. "No talent at all."

"Nonsense," said Holford, but his single word sounded like the usual automatic disclaimer, as though his inner thoughts were far away.

After dinner the four sat for a while in the hotel lounge, but eventually Holford decided that Lynda must go up to her room. "You mustn't overdo it," he advised.

Lynda rose immediately like a child bidden to remember her bedtime. "I shall see you both to-morrow before you leave." She held out her hand first to Holford, then to Duncan. Rianna had the ludicrous notion that Lynda would have enjoyed the gesture much more if the two men had kissed her hand in the Italian fashion.

"I shall come to see you," promised Holford, "but Duncan will be busy aboard the yacht."

"And of course, you also, Rianna." Lynda swung round to the other girl.

"Yes, I shall be here tomorrow morning about ten o'clock," Rianna answered. She had already received her instructions from Holford.

It fell to Duncan to escort Rianna home, although she protested that she could easily take a taxi.

"If you don't mind walking, I'll walk with you," he offered. "The night is fine and starry." He glanced up at the ink-blue sky. "Could be even a night made for romance. But I don't suppose you're feeling in a very romantic mood, considering what you've taken on."

"You mean looking after Mrs. Patterson – Lynda? Oh, that's only for a very short time. Holford said his villa would soon be ready. Besides, when she's better and stronger, she might prefer to stay in the hotel."

"Oh, she won't mind where she stays – as long as it's reasonably close to Holford," Duncan said grimly.

"But isn't she married? Is her husband in England?" The thought flashed through Rianna's mind that Lynda might be divorced.

"She's a widow," was Duncan's terse answer.

"Oh, I see. That's sad for her." In spite of her growing antipathy to Lynda, Rianna felt a stab of compassion for a girl, probably no more than twenty-six or twenty-eight, who had already lost her husband.

"Yes, I suppose it's sad, but actually – in my opinion, that is – Jack Patterson was much too good for her."

"You knew him, then?" queried Rianna.

"Well, of course. Jack was in our team. He was drowned last year – when we were diving in the Pacific."

"Oh!" Rianna gasped with shock and momentarily faltered in her step. Duncan put out a hand to steady her. "I – I didn't realise – I didn't know the name of the – the man who was lost."

For some distance she and Duncan walked along in silence. At last he said, "I'm sorry, Rianna, I didn't mean to give you a shock. I thought you knew."

"Holford said she was the wife of one of his team in the past – he didn't say she was a widow. So of course he feels rather responsible for her?"

"Responsible!" Duncan's voice echoed so harshly in the narrow street that a prowling cat tore away in terror. "Oh, he's certainly made himself responsible for her future. She'll eat him before she's finished with him," he declared emphatically.

"Has she any children?"

"One. A boy. About five years old now, I suppose. She's evidently left him at home in England, probably with relatives – grandmother or someone like that."

"And I suppose she's come here for a long holiday – to be with Holford as much as she can?" Rianna did not realise that her voice had become small and forlorn.

"I suppose that's the size of it – though she knows full well that during most of the summer he wouldn't have too much time to spend with her. In these waters it's our busy time. We have to wait until about now or early April for the water to warm up and we can't do much diving after about the middle of October."

When she and Duncan arrived at what she now called the "hole in the wall", the gate that led to Casa Rosa's courtyard, she thanked him for escorting her and hoped he'd have a pleasant trip to the Egadi islands.

For answer he bent and kissed her lightly on the cheek.

"Goodnight, Rianna – my sweet," he whispered.

Martin was reading a magazine when Rianna entered the sitting room.

"What was the panic about?" he asked.

She slumped into the chair opposite and began to explain briefly, but carefully omitting Lynda's surname.

"So I thought I'd let her have my room and I'll sleep in yours while you're away."

"What happens when I come back?"

"Oh, it's only for a day or two. Holford expects his villa to be ready when you all return from the Egadis."

"Then it didn't amount to much in the end," was Martin's comment. "Signora Offredi seemed to think it was a matter of life and death. Did you have dinner with Holford and this girl?"

"Yes. Duncan came in, too – and brought me home."

Martin smiled at his sister. "Duncan seems to like squiring you."

"Only because I happen to be handy – sister of one of his teammates. Did you see those chairs and table that arrived?"

"Yes. How did they get here? Did you order them?"

"No. Holford sent them." She frowned in dismay. "Oh, heavens! I forgot to thank him."

"You mean he sent them as a present?"

"Actually, I'm not sure. I can offer to pay anyway."

Martin rubbed his chin thoughtfully. "If he means them as a gift, I wonder what he wants in return."

"That sounds mercenary. Is he like that?" she queried.

"I shouldn't have thought so, but you never know –"

"Well, I'm off to bed," Rianna decided. "Goodnight."

In her room, kicking off her shoes, hanging up her clothes and brushing her hair, Rianna had more than enough to think about. The situation had entirely changed. Then an illuminating idea claimed her attention. What was the situation before it was changed by the arrival of one of Holford's friends?

Rianna was reluctant to face that question, for she knew that with every meeting with Holford, the possibility, even the probability, of falling hopelessly in love with him had been growing with mounting strength. Perhaps Lynda's arrival out of the blue would effectively damp down any vain hopes that Rianna might have been inclined to cherish.

CHAPTER THREE

"WHAT time does Holford expect you to join him?" asked Rianna next morning when Martin was making his preparations to leave.

"About ten o'clock at the harbour, he said."

"But he's coming here this morning to bring Lynda. Can't he take you then?"

Martin hesitated and frowned. "No. He may be delayed or change his plans. I have my instructions and I must show him that I obey him as the leader."

Rianna smiled affectionately at her brother. "You're quite right. He'll know that he can always rely on you. Good luck. If you see any coral lying about at the bottom of the sea, bring me a piece."

"Or pieces of eight. Or small treasure chests that no one else has clapped eye on for two thousand years. Very well. Good-bye – and don't let this invalid girl take up too much of your time."

He had been gone half an hour or so before Holford and Lynda arrived. Signora Offredi ushered them through the passage and across the courtyard of the Casa Rosa.

Rianna was already at the door to greet them. "I hope you're not feeling too tired this morning?" she ventured to Lynda, who sighed as she allowed herself to be guided to an easy chair in the sitting room.

Holford returned to his car to bring in Lynda's suitcases.

"I've left a couple of my suitcases at the hotel," Lynda explained. "If I need anything out of them, perhaps you could go and bring me what I want?" Her words were addressed to Rianna, who was staring in surprise at the number of cases which Lynda had brought with her. Four cases, a hatbox, several overnight bags – Rianna was mentally wondering where she would stow all Lynda's possessions in this little Casa Rosa.

"We shall be away at the islands for not more than four days, I think," Holford said to Rianna. "Lynda only needs rest and quiet. I'm sure she won't be a trouble to you."

"I'm glad to be able to help you," she returned. "I hope everything goes well on the trip." Her glance fell on one of the chairs sent yesterday. "By the way, many thanks for sending the chairs and the table. They'll be most useful and I shouldn't have known where to buy such things. There was no bill with them. Will you let me have it?"

Holford stared at her and his eyes were like blue fire. "Of course not. You – and Martin – need some degree of comfort. It's only a very trivial affair, anyway. Use them and enjoy them." He smiled at her and she found herself clinging to the door frame for support, as she watched him disappear along the passage through the *pensione*.

So the chairs and table were a gift and now she also wondered, as Martin had, if some return might have to be made in the future. Then another idea occurred to her. Had these items been bought for Lynda's use? Or even as a tangible reward for her help in taking Lynda for a few days?

Rianna gave up the puzzle and attended to making Lynda comfortable. "What would you like to do? My room is ready for you if you want to lie on the bed. Or would you prefer to sit out in the courtyard?"

Lynda smiled vaguely. "I'm being a frightful trouble to you, but I really will try to be good and not cause any bother. If you could find me a comfortable chair, I'll sit out in the courtyard for a while."

Rianna took out one of the armchairs, arranged cushions and settled Lynda with a rug over her knees. "How's that?"

Lynda nodded. "Thank you. But you'll come and talk to me, won't you? I get so bored when I'm alone."

Rianna thought that for at least a morning she could idle with this demanding young invalid. After that – well, she would have to be tactful and try to do some of her work.

So now she took out notebooks and maps of Sicily, placed them on the new table Holford had given her, but did not ostentatiously start working.

"Have you visited Sicily before?" she asked Lynda.

"No, this is my first visit. I'd heard so much about it and the lovely climate for most of the year that I felt I had to come."

"I'm hoping to explore a good many parts of the island while I'm here," Rianna said. "Sort of business and pleasure combined."

"Oh, yes, you write travel pieces. I remember now. Holford praised you to the skies."

Rianna found this rather difficult to believe, but she merely smiled deprecatingly. "I'm not that excellent – yet. Martin, my brother, and I work together. I do most of the writing. He takes film or still photographs and we sell the results wherever we can."

"Are you staying here long?" queried Lynda.

"In Marsala, do you mean? I shall make this place my base, of course. That's why we've taken this little house for the summer. Martin will of course stay with Holford and the other men for the whole season." She saw no reason to disclose to this other girl that Martin had not yet been fully accepted by Holford.

"Your brother is one of Holford's team?"

"Yes. This is his first season with a team of divers."

"Oh, I see. And you'll be staying here quite a long time." Lynda's blue-grey eyes glinted hard as pebbles.

"Yes, I shall remain with Martin."

"What does he do in the team? What is his special line?"

Rianna hesitated slightly before replying, but saw no way other than the truth. "He's a cameraman. Holford's previous man is still recovering from an accident. He was involved in a fire, I believe, and isn't yet fit for diving."

Lynda was silent for a few moments. Then she said, "Holford is not very lucky in his cameramen." The sadness in her voice touched Rianna with sympathy, but she decided it was best not

47

to mention that she knew of Lynda's loss.

"I'll go in and make some coffee." Rianna promised after a minute or so. "I'm not a marvellous cook, but I can make omelettes. Would that be all right for lunch?"

"No, just a glass of milk and a biscuit for me, please."

The rest of the day passed reasonably smoothly from Rianna's point of view. Lynda rested on the bed after lunch, woke up about five, put on fresh make-up and a dress of pale green chiffon.

"What a pretty dress!" commented Rianna. "You look like a water nymph."

"I suppose we have to amuse ourselves in the evening as best we can – without men," said Lynda. "In a way, I felt it would be better for me if I stayed in the hotel, but Holford wouldn't hear of it. Oh, I don't mean to sound unkind, for you've been so good to me," she apologised quickly. "But it's so dull to spend the evenings without some entertainment."

"We might perhaps go to a cinema," Rianna suggested. "It isn't necessary usually to understand the language perfectly to follow most films."

Lynda frowned slightly. "No, I think not. Films often make my head ache."

"Would you like to have dinner at one of the hotels?" was Rianna's next suggestion. "The one where you were staying or the Umberto?"

"That would be more lively than sitting in the dark in a cinema," agreed Lynda. "Yes, we'll do that."

Rianna thought it wiser not to choose the Bolzano, in case Holford might assume that Lynda was trying to return to that hotel, so she ordered a taxi to take them to the Umberto. So far, she was not very well acquainted with other hotels in the town.

The two girls were shown to a corner table which afforded a view of most of the restaurant. Lynda's gaze roamed over the diners slowly and steadily like a searchlight beam. Rianna ordered from the menu, suggesting the lightest and tastiest dishes for her companion, who seemed quite indifferent to food.

"Nobody you know here, I suppose?" Lynda queried after

48

they had finished their second courses.

"No. I've been here only once – and then only for Martin and me to meet Holford here."

But after dinner in the lounge, a small party of men and women came close to where Rianna and Lynda were sitting and one young man asked if he might take one of the spare chairs. Then instant recognition lit his features and he bowed to Rianna. "The *signorina* from England? You are here with Signor Sinclair?"

Rianna recognised him as one of the men she had been introduced to on that first evening, but she did not remember his name. Introductions were, however, effected and after a few moments he returned to his companions.

"Who is the dark girl?" queried Lynda.

"Her name is Emilia Cavallini. She's the daughter of one of the chief wine-makers here. Beautiful, isn't she?"

Lynda's mouth tightened a little. "I suppose so. Rather a flashy type, but then most Italian girls are."

Rianna was careful to make no comment. Yet she was irritated by Lynda's unwillingness to see or admit Emilia's lovely elegance.

Then the young man, Enrico, returned after a few minutes to invite Rianna and Lynda to join his companions. More introductions followed and Lynda almost immediately became more animated. Even so, Rianna, comparing her and Emilia, reflected that Lynda with her fair looks and pale face, the delicate green dress, was almost extinguished by the pulsing vitality of Emilia, wearing tonight a simply cut dress of Italian silk in riotous patterns of flame, rose and amber.

"You are deserted by all your menfolk?" Emilia asked suddenly.

"Yes," Lynda answered immediately. "They have all gone away to the islands to look for treasure."

There was a general laugh at this remark and Lynda seemed disconcerted for the moment.

"Not really treasure." Rianna came to the rescue. "They're doing some diving exercises from the yacht. They will be back in a few days."

49

The conversation became general, both in English and Italian, and Lynda congratulated Emilia on her excellent English.

"I am glad you find it tolerable," answered Emilia, with a cool smile. "Of course I had an English governess and, too, some of my family are English." After the faintest pause, she asked, "And you speak Italian?"

Lynda shook her head hastily. "Hardly a word, I'm afraid."

Rianna noticed that Lynda had the grace to blush a little at this confession, realising that she had perhaps been patronising to the Italian girl.

The young man, Enrico, asked Emilia if she would like to dance. When Emilia declined, he turned towards Lynda and repeated his invitation.

She rose at once. Rianna asked quickly, "Lynda, do you think you ought to dance? You're not very fit yet."

Lynda laughed, a little trilling laugh that had neither mirth nor merriment in it. "I shan't come to any harm, I'm quite sure, with – Enrico."

"Then don't overtire yourself," warned Rianna.

"She is not strong?" queried Emilia, when Lynda and her partner had reached the door to the ballroom.

"She has been ill recently and has not yet fully recovered, I think," replied Rianna.

"Tell me about the work you and your brother do," invited Emilia.

Rianna complied, revealing only the facts that Martin would wish her to disclose and not touching on some of the projects they had in mind for the future.

The men in the party were engrossed in their own business talk and Rianna warmed to this beautiful Italian girl who could probably at any moment command a dozen admirers to dance attendance on her.

In return, she told Rianna something of the background of her father's wine business. "I believe you are to take a tour of our establishment soon?"

"Yes. When it can be arranged conveniently. No hurry." Secretly, Rianna would have liked to inspect the Cavallini vaults now, while the men were away at the island, but how could she leave Lynda to her own devices? Rianna had promised Holford to look after the girl and she could not go back on her word. As if to confirm the necessity of Rianna's vigilance, Lynda returned with Enrico. She looked paler than ever, although she declared she was all right when Rianna asked, "Are you tired? Do you want to go?"

"No, no. Please don't fuss."

All the same, after another twenty minutes or so, Rianna said firmly that she and Lynda must leave.

In the taxi back to the Casa Rosa, Lynda sulked in her corner. "All I needed was a rest in between," she said petulantly. "I could have gone on dancing half the night if you hadn't stopped me."

"It might be better to wait a week or so before you dance half the night," retorted Rianna. "Holford will be most displeased if he returns and finds you worse than when he went away."

"Yes, of course. I must get well for Holford's sake," murmured Lynda.

For Holford's sake. The words bit into Rianna's mind. What was the real bond between Lynda and Holford, apart from the fact that he was solicitous about her immediate future since she had been widowed? Was he in love with Lynda?

But there was no one available who could answer these questions that floated through Rianna's mind and in the meantime, she must exert her strength to help Lynda to better health.

During the next couple of days Lynda seemed not only much brighter but more amenable to Rianna's suggestions and warnings. The two girls spent some of the morning hours wandering around the shops, lunched at a restaurant or open-air café, then returned to the Casa Rosa for a siesta, during which Rianna occupied herself with itineraries and plans for her various journeys later in the spring and summer.

But it was the evenings when Lynda became restless and longed for the bright lights and gaiety.

"We can't go to the Hotel Umberto every night," Rianna pointed out with a smile, "or we shall become known as two notorious

English girls who frequent the place without escorts."

"We might meet Enrico – or some of the others, all those men hovering around that Italian girl."

"I doubt if they happen to go to the same place every night. Try to settle down for another couple of nights. By that time Holford and the others will return and you can ask him – or tell him – what you'd like to do."

Lynda smiled sweetly and Rianna noticed how the lines of discontent vanished from the girl's face when it was illumined by a sincere smile. "Yes, you're right, of course. I'm an ungrateful wretch after all you've done for me. I really will be patient."

Rianna began to wonder if she had misjudged Lynda. It could be that the shock of being widowed at so early an age had thrown the girl off balance, making her dissatisfied with her life and not knowing how to plan it. Discontent had led to illness, for it was obvious that with so delicate a frame she was not at all strong.

Rianna reflected that she was allowing Duncan's remarks about Lynda to influence her own judgment. In future she would use more tact and gentleness in dealing with the girl.

On the morning of the day when Holford and his team were expected to return to Marsala, Rianna suggested, "Shall we spend the day down at the shore? We can potter about on the beaches, have lunch somewhere and then wait at the harbour for the *Celestina* to come in."

"Yes, that sounds ideal," agreed Lynda, and promptly returned to the bedroom to change her dress, emerging half an hour later wearing a new trouser suit of hyacinth blue with a white organza blouse. Rianna was brushing a cream jacket to wear over her black and green tricel dress.

"That's a nice outfit," she remarked to Lynda.

"Yes. I thought it as well to bring a good stock of clothes with me. You can't be sure of finding what you want in places like this."

After lunch, the two girls strolled to the harbour. "There's a café near by," pointed out Rianna, "where we can sit as long as we like and we'll be able to watch for the *Celestina* when she arrives."

The afternoon wore on and there was no sign of the yacht. Rianna ordered endless cups of coffee, small cakes, ices for Lynda. At five o'clock Lynda said agitatedly, "Something's happened! I know it has!" She ran out of the café enclosure down towards the harbour wall. Rianna stayed only to pay the waiter and then followed.

Lynda stared across the dark sapphire sea and her lips trembled. "I know in my bones when something awful has happened. I did that other time – oh, God! Don't let Holford be taken from me as well!" she whimpered.

Rianna put a comforting arm around Lynda's shoulders. "There could be a most simple explanation. They've decided to stay another day – or perhaps they arrived earlier and we didn't see them."

"Then look for the yacht. You know what it looks like and its name. See if it's here."

It was true that Rianna could not see any craft that resembled the *Celestina.*

She thought for a few moments, deciding what course to take. In a short space of time Lynda might become hysterical.

"I think we should take a taxi to Holford's hotel and see if he has arrived," she suggested calmly.

Without a word Lynda allowed herself to be shepherded into a taxi, but she buried her face in her hands and sobbed throughout the short journey.

Rianna hurried into the hotel and there in the far corner of the lounge were Holford, Duncan, Martin and Jeffrey – the whole lot of them lolling at their ease and drinking Martinis.

"Holford!" exclaimed Lynda in a shaky voice, and promptly collapsed into his arms.

The other men huddled around her. "What on earth has happened?" asked Holford blankly.

Rianna said tersely, "We planned to greet your arrival at the harbour. I'm not sure that we had flags or floral garlands with us, but somehow we seemed to have missed the great arrival."

Holford stared at her. "But we came in hours ago. How could

53

we possibly know of your intentions?"

"True. It was just a whim on our part – or perhaps I should say, *my* part. It was my suggestion and Lynda liked it. When you didn't arrive and we couldn't see the yacht, she suspected some accident had happened."

"It wasn't a very good idea, apparently," he muttered in a low, tense voice. "It's very important that Lynda shouldn't be upset by – by suspected accidents."

"I understand that." She met Holford's glance with her own and hoped he was not too blinded by resentment to see the indignation in her eyes. "Perhaps you should have told me –" She allowed her voice to trail off, realising that all the other men were listening. Duncan rose and called a waiter who a few moments later brought a glass of brandy for Lynda, who drank it thankfully and tried to compose herself.

"I'm sorry I made a scene," she murmured. "I'm all right now."

Jeffrey had ordered Rianna a vermouth and she was glad of a drink to steady her nerves. No one had thought to ask about her apprehension when her only brother was on board a yacht that had apparently failed to arrive at the expected time.

"And how have you managed while we've been away?" asked Holford.

Rianna knew that he was only trying to make casual conversation to bridge the awkward situation, but there was a faint tinge of patronising in his tone, as though he were home from his labours in the City and enquiring how the little woman had spent her day.

"Lynda and I managed to occupy our time quite happily," she answered acidly, "without masculine assistance."

The other three men remained silent and carefully looked away from Holford, although Duncan caught Rianna's eye. In her turn she, too, looked hastily away, for she saw what Duncan was thinking – that Holford had asked for that tart reply.

Martin jumped in quickly with, "I could probably stay a night in the *pensione* next door to us if you don't want Lynda moved." He turned towards Holford.

Holford frowned. "No, I think Lynda had better stay the night here. I'll arrange for a room." He turned towards Rianna with an elaborate show of chilly politeness. "Would you be so kind as to pack a few overnight things for Lynda when you go back? Martin will bring them here to save you trouble."

"Certainly." She flung the word at him as she rose and moved towards Lynda to ask what the latter needed.

"Tomorrow the villa I've rented will be ready and Lynda can transfer there."

Rianna felt the cold exclusion of herself in Holford's tone. But it was not until two days later when the various transfers of baggage had been completed and Lynda was installed in the Villa Aurelia that Rianna received the full force of Holford's strictures.

She and Martin had gone there for a house-warming cocktail party. Duncan and Jeffrey had transferred from their hotels and were now joined by the remaining member of the team, Steve, who would be responsible for first-aid and medical attention when necessary.

"Holford always prefers to have most of his team under one roof when we're starting a season's dives," Duncan had told her at the beginning of the evening.

"Yes, I can see the point of that. But Martin? Does Holford want him here, too?"

"Evidently not for the time being," answered Duncan. "Otherwise he would probably have said so."

Rianna was filled with resentment. So this was one more move to thrust her out from the circle of the team. Holford need not have allowed her to rent the Casa Rosa for the next six months. Why couldn't he have been more frank with her about his plans and intentions? She foresaw that in a week or two Martin would be spending most of his time at the Villa Aurelia when the team was not out in the yacht.

Lynda had apparently installed herself as the hostess and to-night was delighted to be surrounded by attentive men. Had she perhaps known of Holford's plan to rent the villa and timed her arrival to coincide? It was possible, Rianna thought, that Lynda knew of Holford's usual methods. Naturally, the move was much better than staying in a hotel, for she had nothing to do except look pretty and appealing, while a housekeeper attended to running the villa and of course provided a modicum of chaperonage for Lynda.

Rianna found herself in an angry, turbulent mood and not in the least inclined to be cordial towards Holford. When she and Martin were on the point of leaving, she realised that Holford reciprocated her own disaccord.

While Martin was saying a last few words to Duncan and the others, Holford drew Rianna out towards the porch of the villa.

"I'm glad you were able to look after Lynda," he said, and for a moment she forgot her resentment in the warmth of his thanks. "But you shouldn't have allowed her to dance the other evening. She was quite exhausted afterwards."

Rianna met his steely glance. "On the contrary, she seemed livened up. I don't think she suffered any ill effects next day."

Holford sighed. "You don't understand," he murmured patiently. "She lives on her nerves and she often claims to be fit when the contrary is the case."

"Then I'm sorry I was foolish enough to allow her to dance with Enrico, but I treated her as a grown woman who had the right to refuse or accept as she chose. I didn't think *I* had the right to act as her nursemaid."

When she had said the words in a low tone and saw Holford's face, she was appalled at her own rashness. In the brief silence she heard his indrawn breath as though he was about to speak, then decided not to say what was in his mind.

"I'm sorry, Holford," she apologised, knowing that she was in the wrong, yet resentful of the fact that she had allowed herself to be put in that position. "I shouldn't have said that, but Lynda –"

"Of course I've no right to ask favours of you," he interrupted, "and Lynda is really my responsibility, but – as a friend – I hoped I could rely on you to extend a small amount of care to a girl who has lost so much. Not only her health, but much more."

56

"I tried to do my best," muttered Rianna. "If there's anything in the future that I can do –" her voice trailed away.

"That's not likely," he snapped. "Naturally you have your own work to do on the island while we're away on the yacht, and I wouldn't want to interfere with that."

There was no opportunity for any further conversation for Martin and Duncan were approaching. Rianna schooled her face into the semblance of a polite smile, murmured goodbyes to the other men as well as Holford, kissed Lynda lightly on the cheek, before marching out of the villa through the small horse-shoe garden to the road.

On the way home she and Martin spoke of trivial topics, but when they were indoors at the Casa Rosa, her brother asked, "Is there anything wrong between you and Holford?"

"No. Why should there be?"

He shrugged. "I just felt that there was some bone of contention between you. You don't dislike him, do you?"

Rianna managed to laugh. "No, of course not. Even if I did, I'd still manage to be friendly with him for your sake. I would certainly not go out of my way to alienate him."

"Good. That's all right then. Only it might worry me if I knew that you two were at loggerheads."

"Don't worry about that. It's merely a matter that he doesn't want me on the yacht or upsetting any of his team in any way." She spoke in her most reassuring tone. Martin must not guess that tonight she had come face to face with the fact that she was ragingly jealous of Lynda, the frail girl who could apparently twist Holford around the proverbial little finger.

What tale had Lynda told Holford about dancing? Why had she needed to mention the subject at all, if not to show Rianna in a faulty light?

Yet, until Lynda's sudden appearance, Rianna had been attracted towards Holford, even if she recognised the fact that he was opposed to Martin's sister having too close a connection with the diving project and regarded her as an encumbrance.

She could easily involve herself in her own plans and tours

and would be glad to discard any particular feeling for Holford that might have been embryonic. He was no more than her brother's employer and naturally she would try to be on good terms with him. But, underlying these brave resolutions, was the secret, haunting knowledge that she was jealous of the regard he paid to another girl, the protection he gave to the fragile Lynda, widow of one of his former comrades. Had he a further obligation towards Lynda than that of employer of her husband?

Already Rianna had recalled several times those words of Lynda's when waiting at the harbour for the yacht to come in – *Don't let Holford be taken from me as well!* It was the possessive phrase *"from me"* that barbed Rianna so acutely.

Rianna determined that as soon as the men went off on their first diving expedition, she would apply herself wholeheartedly to her own films and articles. No further decisions had apparently been made as to when she was to visit the wine-making establishment, so she would go off to Trapani or Segesta or somewhere and endeavour to rid her mind of the troublesome thoughts of Holford.

"All the tests I took off the island seemed to satisfy Holford," Martin had already told her, so now she asked when he thought the team would be leaving.

"Not until the day after tomorrow. Holford is waiting for some special air cylinders."

"Whereabouts is the first dive?" she queried.

Martin grinned. "I'm not supposed to tell you, but since anyone can see the yacht wherever it happens to be, I can say that we're sailing south-east more or less towards Selinunte. That's a part of the coast where thousands of Roman amphorae have been found at one time or other, but that isn't our particular interest. Holford would be more excited if he could trace remnants of old ships."

"Wrecks? Sunken ships?"

"Well, remains of a Punic ship were found some time ago. He thinks it possible that others – or at least, other historical ships might also be there."

Rianna smiled. "If only you could locate them."

"That's it. The bottom of the sea knows how to cover up its treasures."

"Then I hope you're the one to make the great discoveries," she said warmly.

CHAPTER FOUR

When Martin went next day to the gymnasium swimming pool where he practised his diving exercises with the other men of the team, Rianna set out in earnest to explore the town of Marsala with her ciné camera. She had told Martin that she would wait until he sailed with the yacht before she went to Trapani or other places where necessarily she would have to stay several nights in hotels.

"We might as well make the fullest use of the Casa Rosa now that we have it," she said.

"I shall probably go to the Villa Aurelia when I leave the gym. Holford may want to brief us for next day."

Rianna made no further comment, reflecting that naturally it would have been much better if Martin also could have stayed in the villa, instead of commuting back and forth to the little Casa.

But today she excluded these unwelcome thoughts and concentrated on filming streets and buildings, small children playing, two women gossiping and an old man with a white patriarchal beard that fell below his capacious waist. By now she had an expert eye for scenic value and the knack of being able to film unobtrusively wherever possible. In a small square close to a church she sat on a seat to write a few notes in her book, marking on a street map the area she had just photographed.

A shadow fell across the page, but she took little notice other than to move a few inches along the seat to give the newcomer more room.

"Am I interrupting you?" queried the voice close to her ear.

She jumped and the ball pen fell from her hand, rolling in

the dust at her feet. "Holford!"

"Sorry if I startled you. I hope I'm not intruding if you're writing up a diary."

She smiled in spite of all her former harsh thoughts about him. This morning his voice was gentle and warm and quite managed to cancel out any hard edges of previous conversations. His voice also had the quality to set her longing for him to continue talking.

"Oh, it's only my notes of where I've been today and the places I've filmed."

"Then you'd better write down the items. I don't want to be blamed for mixing up one street with another."

She gave him a ready smile, then turned quickly to her notebook lest he should see an expression in her eyes that might be too revealing.

He remained silent while she jotted down particulars. When she closed the notebook, he said, "Rianna, I must apologise for the way I spoke last night. It was unjust and quite unpardonable. I can only say that I was unduly worried about Lynda and that I—"

"Don't think about it any more," she cut in. "I was just as bad. I hit back and I didn't mean to."

Holford laughed. "You've certainly shown me that you're a girl who can give as good as she gets!"

Rianna gazed at her hands in her lap. "My father taught me to stand up to a few blows that life might deal me. Maybe I've sometimes taken his advice too literally."

"Then when you're ready, come and have lunch with me."

She agreed readily, not daring to ask him how he came to be roaming about the streets of Marsala when his team were hard at work with their swimming and diving exercises. Nor could she mention Lynda or enquire how he had managed to evade lunching at his own villa.

Holford guided Rianna to a restaurant in a small street where a sign illustrating two fishermen hauling in their nets indicated that seafood was a speciality of the house.

When she picked up the menu, Rianna said, "I haven't the

least idea of the names of the fish, so you'd better choose for me. In any case, I expect they're fish that we never see in our Northern waters."

"You'd be frightened by the looks of some of them!" he told her.

"I've already seen fearsome specimens on slabs in the markets. Not only here in Sicily, but elsewhere. In Spain, for instance, and the Canaries. Yet it's only a matter of habit and what we're accustomed to seeing in our own country. You must meet some odd fish when you're diving."

"It's one of the pleasures of exploring the underwater world. You've probably seen films of divers floating through shoals of multi-coloured fish, but to be down there among the creatures is unbelievable."

"Do they attack divers? I thought some fish were harmful."

"Plenty are harmful. Sting-rays and stonefish. Then there are sea-urchins which are not exactly fish, but can be an abominable nuisance with their spines."

"Have you met sharks?"

"Once or twice. In the Pacific, that was. Sharks are more likely to attack divers on the surface than when submerged, so the best way to avoid attention is to lie quietly down below – rather easier said than done. One's instinct is to rise as quickly and safely as you can."

A plate of fish was served to Rianna. Delicate flakes of a creamy colour were coated with a piquant sauce and she pronounced the flavour as delicious.

As the meal progressed through aubergines in a sweet-sour sauce and pork fritters with red peppers to a sweet flavoured with pine-nut, Rianna encouraged Holford to tell her more about the environment of his work.

"Perhaps you could say that it's a slow-motion world as though you were on another planet where time and movement are different. It's like a multi-coloured dream, full of fantasy and beauty and softness."

"I thought it was always dark when you went to any depth," she interposed.

62

"That depends on many things at the time – the weather, the climate, how far down you go. At some points you're in a silence of blues and greens, but there are times when I think of the lines – 'A ceiling of amber, a pavement of pearl'."

"Oh, yes, Matthew Arnold's *Forsaken Merman*."

"It's not all pearly floor, of course. Often it's sand which shifts about from day to day. I think what appeals to me so much in diving is that the laws of gravity are reversed and you can float about in all directions. It's almost like being a bird in the air, except that you don't need wings."

"And you don't mind the risks?" she queried.

"There are always risks," he answered gravely. "The sea is not naturally man's element and it's completely unforgiving if you're careless or imprudent or plain ignorant. That's why I've made Martin take such severe tests. I have to be sure that he understands the dangers, both to himself and to others. We never dive alone, but in pairs, so that each man is partly responsible for his companion. They can help each other if trouble arises. No man is ever left to fend for himself or believe that he's alone."

"But in the case of Martin when he's photographing, isn't he the odd man out if there are two others of the team?"

"No. He still has someone accompanying him, even though his mate has certain other work to do. But Martin – or any other cameraman – is always completely sure that if a difficulty arises, someone will come to his aid."

Rianna was thoughtful for a few moments, remembering that a former cameraman, Lynda's husband, Jack, had been drowned. But since she did not know the true circumstances of that accident, she could not mention the matter now to Holford.

When they were ready to leave the restaurant, Rianna assumed that Holford would bid her goodbye and leave her to continue her wanderings with the camera, but he suggested various quarters of the town which might be interesting.

"I think you might get lost without a guide," he offered.

"I'll be glad to have a *cicerone*," she answered. She was now enjoying this day to the full with no shadows to cast gloom anywhere. Yet at the back of her mind was a vague fear that sooner or later she would make some careless remark that would destroy this new-found harmony between her and Holford.

He guided her along tiny streets, mere openings between buildings, where she would never have intruded; he showed her monuments to important personages who had played their part in history, such as Garibaldi, and the small, solitary figures to be found in back streets, men who had been commemorated for some contribution to the arts or sciences.

From the top of a triumphal arch that straddled one of the main streets she was able to look down into a cloistered courtyard with trees and flower beds in the centre. Later, he conducted her through short cuts to the public gardens where seats were placed in the shade of chestnut trees and one could watch water from the fountains trickle over a miniature waterfall into a small lake.

"Thank you, Holford," she murmured, when she had finished noting down in her book the various camera shots she had taken. "I've spent a wonderful day in Marsala and I've recorded the happiest souvenirs."

It was at that moment that his mood suddenly became sombre. "Souvenirs," he echoed. "Well, at some time in the future, when you show the film, you'll be able to say — 'Oh, yes, Marsala in Sicily. Now who was the man who toured me around?'"

"I'm hardly likely to forget that man's name," she said lightly.

"Quite a lot in our lives has to be forgotten. Come on, it's time we went home." He rose suddenly as though to thrust aside any more disturbing thoughts and at the exit of the gardens called a taxi.

The Casa Rosa was in the same direction as Holford's Villa Aurelia, so it was obvious that he would drop Rianna at her door and continue. Yet outside the *pensione*, he paid off the taxi and accompanied Rianna into her courtyard.

"I wanted to speak to Martin if he's back," he said.

But Martin had apparently not returned.

"Is there any message I can give my brother when he comes?" asked Rianna.

Holford hesitated a moment. "Only that I'd like him to be down at the harbour not later than noon. He knows which part of the harbour."

Even then, Rianna expected him to take his leave, but he sat in one of the chairs he had himself provided and lit a small cigar.

Slightly flustered by his unexpected reluctance to part company with her, Rianna offered coffee. "It won't take long," she promised.

He nodded and she rushed indoors to the kitchen, dumping her camera and handbag on an adjacent table. Did he expect her to ask him to stay to dinner? Hurriedly she mentally surveyed what she could offer. Not much – eggs for omelettes, tinned soups, a few beans, and a little smoked ham.

When she took the tray of coffee out to the courtyard she asked, "Would you like to have dinner here? I could knock up something quickly – if you're not too fussy."

He gave her a teasing glance that unsteadied her for the moment. "And what if I say I'm the most pernickety man over my food?"

"Then you should never consent to take pot luck." Then, in case he might think she was choking him off, she added quickly, "But think what you might miss!"

He laughed. "I'll take you up on that on some future occasion and test your cookery skill. But it's time I was going now."

He rose as soon as he had finished the coffee. She accompanied him across the courtyard to the gate in the wall. He turned towards her with a smile that lifted her heart.

"Was it a good day?" he queried.

"I've enjoyed it very much," she answered as calmly as she could.

"We must become tourists and go sightseeing again some time." He held her hand in a warm clasp and his touch did nothing to soothe her nerves.

He was outside the gate and had taken a couple of steps before she remembered to wish him "Bon voyage! Hope the trip goes well."

He nodded and walked away up the narrow street, his lithe

figure moving with easy grace. When he turned the corner he did not glance back as she had half expected, but then he was not to know that she was standing there outside the gate, lost in a cocoon of fantasy.

She shut the gate, walked across the courtyard and sank down in what she now termed "one of Holford's chairs". She finished the pot of coffee, but was too lazy to prepare dinner. She would wait until Martin returned. For the time being she was content to sit musing, entranced by the fact that even if Holford had come across her by accident earlier in the day, he had chosen to spend the rest of it with her, shepherding her in and out of the more picturesque spots and finally accompanying her home. He had even hinted at further expeditions when the opportunity offered, so he could not dislike her quite so much as at first she had feared.

Increasing darkness brought the realisation that the hour was becoming late – and Martin had not yet returned. She decided to have a meal in the *pensione* to save cooking for herself. Obviously Martin would have eaten elsewhere.

When he came home shortly before ten o'clock, she was back in the Casa Rosa and immediately gave him Holford's message about the timing for tomorrow.

"Oh, you saw him, then?"

She recounted briefly how she had spent the day. "He was most useful, taking me to out-of-the-way spots I'd never have known for myself."

"When we were at the swimming pool this morning, he asked me what you were doing today and I told him I thought you were giving Marsala the 'Rianna Derwent treatment'. He left us fairly early, having given us our drill and exercise programme. So I suppose he knew the likely places where you might be photographing."

Rianna laughed. "Marsala is rather larger than a village. I wonder he could find me." She almost hugged herself with delight at this revelation that Holford had actually sought her out.

"I went back with the others after lunch to Holford's villa. Jeffrey and Steve went aboard the yacht to check some of the equipment and then they joined Duncan and me for dinner at the villa."

"Wasn't Lynda there?" Rianna queried casually.

"No. Apparently she'd been invited to spend the day with the Cavallinis. I wish I had," added Martin ruefully. "I'd have enjoyed an afternoon with the lovely Emilia, but no such luck."

His last sentence floated over Rianna's consciousness almost without meaning. The truth had been hurled at her in a shattering blow. So Lynda was not available during the day and Holford had contented himself with Rianna's company instead. Her euphoria vanished now, leaving her with mixed feelings of bruised pride and self-contempt that she had been so foolish as to imagine that she was the kind of girl whom Holford would choose as a companion if Lynda or someone like her were available.

It was perhaps fortunate that for the next hour she had to occupy herself with checking that Martin had everything he needed for the trip tomorrow. Most of his equipment was already on board the yacht, but there were several odds and ends that Rianna helped him to collect.

"You think that Holford has really accepted you as cameraman after all those tests?" she asked. "Is he satisfied?"

"He ought to be. He gave me some gruelling tests," answered Martin grimly. "When we were off the Egadi islands, he pretended to be in trouble. Actually, I didn't know whether he was, or only shamming. But I had to do my rescue stuff and bring him to the surface. Fortunately the water wasn't deep enough for us to have to stop for decompression, so up we came without panic."

"But he was only shamming?"

"Yes. When we were hauled on board, he laughed, but I didn't see the joke just then, although afterwards he told Duncan and Jeffrey that I'd passed the 'guardian angel' test O.K."

In the dull despair that now enveloped her, Rianna felt gratified that Martin had so far been able to convince Holford of his competency. She need not worry on that score, but she must keep a firm control over her own emotions so that no disruption could possibly occur between her brother and his employer.

When Holford had directed Martin to be at the harbour next day not later than noon, Rianna had intended to accompany her brother and see the men off on their first diving expedition of the season, but she shrank from meeting Holford again so soon. She guessed that Lynda might also be there at the harbour and she did not want to be delayed in beginning her own journey to Trapani northwards along the coast.

Next morning she and Martin left the Casa Rosa together. "I'll join up with the others at Holford's villa," Martin said.

"All right. I have to catch an early bus because I want to break the journey at one of the towns en route, so that I can go down to the coast."

"We ought to think about hiring a car for ourselves, chiefly so that you could get yourself around the island without having to depend on public transport."

"Yes, I think it's a good idea," replied Rianna, "but there was no point in hiring it too soon before either of us had made any definite plans."

The taxi stopped at the Villa Aurelia and Martin alighted.

"Shall I give your love to Holford?" he asked lightly. "Or perhaps to Duncan? He has a soft spot for you."

"Jeffrey might be safer."

"Oh, he's a hermit. Says he never knows what to say to girls."

Rianna laughed. When Jeffrey had come to the Casa Rosa to mend the cooking stove and subsequently taken her to lunch, he had completely lost his shyness, she thought.

"Have a good trip and take care of yourself," she counselled Martin.

"You, too. Don't lose yourself in the mountains."

Rianna left the Trapani bus at a point about halfway between that town and Marsala. A minor road went towards the coast and she was anxious to do this part of the journey on foot; she had calculated the distance as about three miles and was quite capable of walking that far, even encumbered with a small overnight bag as well as her cameras.

Covering the distance to the shore was no problem and she

68

took several sequences of the coastal scenery, the small off-shore islands and then explored the village of Birgi. By the time she had finished filming and eaten some biscuits, cheese and fruit she had brought with her, she knew she ought to return to the main road in order not to miss the early evening bus to Trapani. But the day had warmed up by now and she realised that even as early as the end of March could be hot by English standards. Nevertheless, she trudged along the road, hoping that some vehicle might be travelling in her direction, but nothing appeared. Of course, it was siesta time and neither man nor beast would stir from choice.

Near the cross-roads a bridge forded the river and she sat on the parapet for a few minutes to rest. Then she saw a man with a donkey coming along the road to the right. He smiled and shouted "*Buon giorno*" followed by a spate of Italian too fast for her to follow.

She moved towards him as he stopped the donkey and asked how far it was to the main road to Trapani and the bus route.

The Italian pursed his lips and finally guessed it was about six kilometres.

"Surely not more than two kilometres," she said slowly in her hesitating Italian.

"No. Six," he said firmly. "Maybe more. Too far to walk. Come with me one kilometre and I take you to my uncle's house. He has a car and can take you all the way to Trapani."

Slightly dubious about this suggestion, Rianna agreed and hoped that she would arrive at her destination. She had booked a room at a Trapani hotel by telephone and did not want to spend the night wandering about rough country roads in such unknown territory. She argued with herself that the bus would already have gone by the time she reached the road, so she might as well accept the man's offer.

Rianna and the young Italian walked at the donkey's pace. At one point the man took her small suitcase and piled it on top of the baskets and panniers and boxes on the donkey's back, but she protested sharply, "Oh, no! He's already carrying enough."

So the man took charge of the case, swinging it easily in his free hand. It was not much more than half a mile along the road when he stopped at a small house and asked her to wait a few minutes while he talked with his uncle.

Eventually he returned, accompanied by an older man with a tanned face and a brigand moustache.

"Trapani!" the older one queried, then he shook his head.

In Italian the young one told her that his uncle was too tired but he would drive Rianna himself. She nodded agreement when she fully understood his words after repetition slowly a couple of times.

The car was so old and rusty that she was surprised it did not fall to pieces on the rough road, but eventually she saw the sign "Trapani" on the outskirts of the town and her driver landed her outside the hotel where she had booked.

When she offered him payment, he at first refused, but she persuaded him eventually to accept rather more than the bus fare would have cost her. His name was Giovanni, he told her, and any time he would be pleased to give her a lift.

In her hotel room, after a bath and change of dress, she laughed quietly at the afternoon's adventure. She must be more careful in future about mistiming buses and it might be worth while to hire a car here in Trapani for a week.

Duncan had recommended the hotel to her and she found it extremely comfortable and the food excellent. She spent the evening working on her notes and recording the filming she had done during the day, including the shots she had taken of Giovanni and his donkey.

Next morning she explored the town of Trapani on its narrow neck of land jutting into the sea. From its seaward points stretched the harbour breakwaters like tentacles and to the south were the salt-beds. It was an easy town to traverse, for one could cut through the streets and emerge on the opposite shore of the peninsula.

She decided to bathe at the Lido San Giuliano, a short distance from the town. Sandy beaches, coloured umbrellas and the cafés open, but there were few bathers actually in the water. Most people apparently preferred to sunbathe and when Rianna entered the water, she knew the reason, for the sea had not yet warmed up as quickly as the land. After a quick swim she was glad to lie in the sun for a while. She took a few shots of the beach scene, then dressed and returned to Trapani.

In the lavender twilight there was little mystery left in the more modern streets with recent buildings, but in the side streets and small squares, the old patrician mansions and the baroque palaces with their ornate façades seemed to assert themselves, challenging the less stylish upstarts towering above them.

Rianna made a note of several views that she would take on another occasion in daylight. On arrival back at her hotel she enquired about hiring a small car on a daily basis, and after a certain amount of bargaining next morning at a local garage, she set off for Erice, an ancient town with cyclopean walls of silvery-grey granite, surmounted by Norman ramparts.

Here the streets became so narrow and were without footpaths that Rianna was forced to abandon the car in a piazza and continue on foot, hoping that no mischievous boys would wreck the vehicle in her absence.

Open doors leading into courtyards gave glimpses of outside staircases decked with masses of vivid flowers in tubs or boxes. Elsewhere she explored a fine collection of medieval towers and castles with battlements.

She lunched at an inn housed in an old converted tower – she told herself that she had never eaten a meal in a dungeon before, where no daylight entered and clusters of small lanterns hung on the walls only seemed to intensify the gloom.

A winding road branching off to the left took her to Cape San Vito, one of the northerly points of the island, and from here she could survey the whole of the huge Gulf of Castellamare, an indigo basin fringed with white towns and the vague mauve shapes of mountains behind them.

She sat on a smooth piece of rock, gazing at the lovely scene around her, and began to work on her notes to accompany the films she had taken. She enjoyed her work, but she missed Martin's companionship. Usually they had gone to places together, chatted about the views, laughed over comic incidents and generally shared the pleasure and the work. Alone, there was no one to point out the best vantage spot or argue about the direction of the light. Rianna's thoughts returned to that day with Holford in Marsala. That was still a day to cherish, even if afterwards she had discovered that he was merely at a loose end.

However strongly she might be attracted towards him, she must try to be sensible and not demand more than he was willing to give.

She was sitting outside the hotel next morning on the small terrace studying her route maps and brochures of various localities, when an English voice said, "Hullo, Rianna! Remember me?"

"Why, Duncan! Where did you spring from?"

"Sicily can be full of surprises. All sorts of gods seemed to have floated here or risen from the sea. Not, of course, that I'm a god," he added hastily.

"But you might just have risen from the sea. Is the diving over?"

"For the time being, yes. We can't do more than a limited amount each day. Then we have to knock off for a few days and start again."

"And Martin? Has he done his work well?"

"Yes, I'm pretty sure of that. He was still on the yacht when I left. He had some developing or film-processing to do."

Rianna was silent for a few moments. Naturally, Duncan had known where she was staying in Trapani, for he had given her the name of the hotel, but she wondered why he had taken the trouble to follow her from Marsala.

"What are your plans for today?" he asked at length. "I don't want to interfere, of course."

She smiled at him. "I suppose I could say that I don't want your company, but it wouldn't be true. I've hired a car and when I'm driving, I find I'm talking to myself all the time."

He grinned at her. "So I can have my uses as a kind of sounding-board?"

"Sounding-boards don't usually talk back – only echo. I'm sure you wouldn't be content with that."

72

"Have you been to Segesta yet?" he asked.

"I was planning to go there today, but I was wondering which was the best road to take."

"This one." He pointed to a minor road that branched off from the main one. "It takes rather longer, but is much more picturesque and probably has less traffic on it."

He drove out of Trapani and after the first few miles she was glad he was at the wheel, for the roads were serpentine over the mountain slopes.

He was still some miles from Segesta when he suggested they should stop and eat their picnic lunch.

"Tramping about over Greek theatres and temple sites is energetic work," he commented, "and if we eat first, we shall be well fortified."

Rianna agreed that this was sensible and they shared the food she had bought in Trapani – small pastry rolls filled with sardines, spicy sausages and thin slices of meat rolled and filled with cheese, breadcrumbs and onion. Almond biscuits finished off the meal and Duncan had purchased two large bottles of wine, a red Corvino and a white Alcamo, both local Trapani wines.

Rianna shook the crumbs from her almond green trouser suit. "Whether I shall be in a fit state to explore temples and theatres after this lot remains to be seen."

"Don't worry yet. You've plenty of walking to do," he warned her.

She found Duncan a pleasant companion and was delighted that apparently Providence had sent him when she was tiring of her own company. Yet when she stood with him inside the unfinished Greek temple and he showed her that the Doric columns had never been completed or smoothed off, she knew she would have preferred to be in the company of Holford.

"I find it a marvel," she said, "that these places can have lasted so long, withstanding battles and destruction of all kinds."

"Earthquakes, too, but this one, I believe, was lost for centuries. Gradually, the earth had heaped itself up all around the columns."

Rianna moved her hand over the rough surfaces of the columns, feeling the warmth of today's sun and remembering that many other hands had fashioned the columns more than two thousand years ago.

She used both her ciné camera and the small hand camera for shots of the temple from different angles. She and Duncan were alone here at the site and she was impressed by the silent grandeur of the pale gold stone and the magnificent proportions of the temple, open to the sky and defying the elements. On the slopes immediately below there were giant prickly pear and lower down the ground was carpeted with flowers, asphodel and marigolds and some small mauve flowers that neither she nor Duncan could identify.

At the Greek theatre farther up the hill, there were a few people scattered about, resting on the tiered stone seats.

"Those who built these places certainly knew how to choose a site," Rianna commented, adjusting her camera to take in the magnificent view of green-clad hills and farther away the mauve heights fading into the clear blue sky. "Apparently there was once a whole city up here on this height, surrounded by walls. People lived here and walked in the streets and came to this arena to watch plays and spectacles – and now there's nothing left except these lovely rows of stone seats."

"Too many barbarians," answered Duncan tersely.

He was in the act of lighting a cigarette and obviously waiting for her to take her various photographs and film shots. She supposed it would be expecting too much to believe that he was as moved by these ancient sites as she was. He had not the same sense of the continuity of history and, besides, his first love was no doubt the sea and its treasures.

She sat on one of the arena seats to write up her notes and after a few minutes Duncan came up from the floor of the theatre to join her.

"You do your work very thoroughly, don't you?" he said.

"If you don't jot down what you've seen and the film shots you've taken, you're in the soup," she answered. "You always kid yourself you can remember, but after a week or so and after you've visited many other places, you're muddled."

74

"How do you process the films here?"

"Martin says he can take mine on the yacht and do them in his spare time."

"Yes, of course. He has to do his own."

"Have you seen any of the underwater work he has done so far?"

"Not yet." After a pause, he said, "You're anxious about him?"

"Only that I very much want him to succeed. It's a new venture for him and I want Holford to be pleased with Martin's work."

Duncan glanced at her, his grey eyes gleaming with amusement and another expression which Rianna could not precisely name. "And do you want Holford to be pleased with your work?"

She looked up, then away across the hilly landscape. "It doesn't really matter to him what my work is like. He doesn't have to try to sell it. That's my job – and Martin's."

"But you'd like his approval?" he persisted.

She smiled, still not looking at him. She was not prepared to confess to Duncan how much she longed for Holford's approbation. She was reluctant to admit the fact even to herself.

"Martin and I have to be judges of our own work," she answered at last as casually as she could. "Sometimes we know it's reasonably good, but there are times when we haven't made the best use of our opportunities."

Duncan stubbed out his cigarette. "I always try to make the best use of *my* opportunities." The oblique glance he gave her was mischievous and philandering at the same time.

She rose quickly and walked down the stone steps to the lower level of the arena. "I must take one or two shots of the ruins of the old city," she said. "Then I expect we must leave."

On the way back to Trapani, Duncan chose the main road from which at intervals Rianna could catch glimpses of the Egadi islands.

"You can see where there's a new road under construction to go straight to the airport at Birgi."

75

"Birgi. Oh, yes. I walked past that place the first day I came here."

"Walked? What were you doing at Birgi?" he wanted to know.

She giggled. "I broke my journey halfway and went down to the coast."

"How did you get to Trapani, then? There's no bus service."

"Oh, I got a lift," she said airily.

"On what? A donkey?"

"Indeed, no. The donkey was already carrying too great a load without my weight. The man took me to a cottage and drove me to Trapani in a very old car."

"Have you written that down in your notebook as one of your Italian incidents?" Duncan queried.

"I can remember that. It would be highly dangerous to jot down everything that happened on my tours. One never knows if the notebook will fall into undesirable hands."

He laughed. "I regard that as a threat – if not an incitement to snatch your notebooks and take them away to have a quiet read and discover all."

In Trapani outside her hotel he told her that he was staying at a small place just off the Corso Italia. "It's only round the from here."

"Thank you for such a pleasant day, Duncan." She knew that she ought to ask him to dinner at her hotel, but she hesitated. She did not want him to jump to hasty conclusions. His immediate rejoinder solved that problem.

"Oh, the day isn't over yet by any means. I thought we might have dinner together at a place I know not far from here. Serves excellent Sicilian food. What about it? You've done all your notes for the day, so you haven't that excuse."

She could hardly refuse. As she showered and then put on a dress of peacock blue jersey, the only one she had brought with her on this short trip, she wondered how far Duncan expected encouragement or whether his casual, flirtatious attitude was his normal one towards most girls.

She brushed out her dark copper hair to its shoulder-length cut and curled the ends under. A touch of green eye-shadow gave her sherry brown eyes a sparkle. Well, she told her reflection in the mirror, nothing was to be gained by moping in her own hotel, so she might just as well enjoy the evening with Duncan.

She was emboldened to try the Arab dish of *kus-kus,* a favourite of the Trapani district, Duncan told her. He began to explain that it was concocted of semolina and fish broth, but she begged, "Don't tell me how it's made or I might be put off."

Baked pasta with tomatoes and aubergines, then a cheese made with saffron and pepper, and finally a delicious ice cream with hazelnuts. At the end Rianna declared that any further mouthful would choke her.

"All delicious dishes," she commented, raising her glass of wine. "How do you manage to know all these places and so much about the island?"

Duncan shrugged. "I'd been here a week or two before you came and I wandered about, sampling places."

After dinner Rianna walked with him along the avenue by the sea-front, a long wide street bordered with palm trees.

"This avenue has a lovely name," she remarked. "I looked it up on the map. The Sea-front of the North Wind – the Tramontana."

"So?" Duncan murmured. "Sometimes I think you've a touch of the Tramontana yourself. You blow a most icy wind over me sometimes."

"Sorry. You must remember that I haven't known you very long."

"Nonsense! That has nothing to do with it. All day I could feel you edging away from me, as though if I touched you you'd scuttle away as fast as a lizard."

She laughed quietly. "I'm not sure that I care for the comparison."

They were in a shadier corner of the promenade at the end where a walled space was provided with seats. Duncan drew her down on to one of the seats and his arm enfolded her against him.

"What is it about me that you dislike?" he queried softly.

77

"But I don't dislike you!" she protested. "I regard you as a friend, a colleague of Martin."

"I find you very attractive. But I expect plenty of men before me have told you that."

"Only two or three," she admitted.

He laughed scornfully. "Two or three dozen more likely. Tell me, Rianna, how many men have loved you?"

"Loved? Or merely professed that they were in love with me?"

"You rate the difference very high?"

"Very high indeed," she assured him gravely.

"Then tell me about the men who have really loved you and what they were like."

She did not answer immediately. When she spoke her voice was perhaps more wistful than she realised. "I've known a few young men," she said. "Few girls arrive at the age of twenty-three without some acquaintance with your sex. But I'm not sure that any of them really loved me. I was not much more than a passing fancy to them."

"And you? Which of them did you love?"

"Oh, none!" she replied quickly. "I haven't yet met the man with whom I might like to spend the rest of my life." Even as she uttered the words, she knew them to be far from the truth, a downright lie, in fact. If Holford ever turned towards her with love in his eyes, she would accept that he was the man.

"That's bad news for me," Duncan was saying. "I was hoping it might be otherwise."

"Why? You're not exactly the constant type, are you?"

"I might be," returned Duncan. "You never know. I've known other girls, but you're different."

Rianna laughed softly. "How unoriginal! Every man says that to the girl of the moment."

"Ah, but you're not just my girl of the moment. I might even want to tie myself down."

"I doubt it!" she said crisply. "You're a born roamer, Duncan. Footloose —"

"But never fancy-free," he interrupted. "And why am I more footloose than Holford? Now there's a constant type for you, if

78

you like. You know, he knew Lynda years ago, before she met Jack Patterson. I don't know whether they were engaged, but perhaps they had a tiff and then afterwards she married Jack."

This new revelation closed around Rianna's heart like an icy covering. "Was she happy with Jack?" she managed to say through stiff lips.

"Not very, I should think. Lynda's a vain, shallow, selfish little creature, always demanding her own way. She probably led old Jack quite a dance. He was easy-going, gave in all the time and let her see that he worshipped her. If Holford isn't careful, she'll do the same to him. Now that she's free of Jack and has met up with Holford again, she'll dig her claws in and never let him go."

Every word that Duncan uttered added to the chill that enveloped Rianna. If Lynda was an old acquaintance, even a former fiancée of Holford, and had now come back so determinedly into his life, what chance had Rianna of achieving more than the status of Martin's sister?

Unconsciously she shivered and Duncan immediately asked solicitously, "Are you cold?"

"Yes, a little." She would have immediately risen to go, but he clasped her in a tight embrace and kissed her lips with considerable fervour.

"I could put a little warmth into you," he whispered. "That red hair of yours doesn't belong to a girl who poses as an ice-maiden."

"Come on, it's time we went back." She freed herself from his grasp. "I'd much prefer it, Duncan, if we could be good friends."

"For the time being," he agreed. "If that's the way you want it."

It was the way she wanted it, but not only for the time being. The last thing she really desired was some complicated relationship with Duncan that would spoil matters for Martin.

Duncan drove her back to Marsala next day, using his own car, for she had surrendered the one she had hired in Trapani. His attitude was easy and matter-of-fact and he gave no sign of being disconcerted by her refusal to take his mild advances too seriously.

It was late afternoon when Duncan drove into the front court-yard of the Villa Aurelia. "You don't mind if I call there first, do you?" he had asked Rianna. "I'd better find out if Holford has fixed up his next diving session. Then I'll drive you to your villa and you can have dinner with me somewhere."

Rianna had agreed, but made private reservations about dining with Duncan that evening.

As she alighted from the car she saw that Holford and Martin were standing in the porch of the villa and they were immediately joined by Lynda, looking ravishing in a pale primrose dress.

"Looks as though we have a reception committee," remarked Duncan as he walked round the front of the car.

In the next hour or so Rianna discovered that the reception turned out to be more in the nature of a storm than a succession of smiles and handshakes.

CHAPTER FIVE

LYNDA was the first to speak. "Dear Rianna, I'm so glad you're back. Did you and Duncan have a good time? We'd no idea you were both going to be away so long. Come along in. You must tell me all about your trip."

Lynda clung on to Rianna's arm and propelled her towards the villa entrance.

Martin smiled and asked, "Taken any good films lately?" but Holford, far from greeting or welcoming her, stood there glowering, his eyes like blue ice.

Rianna wondered what latest crime she had committed to account for this stormy atmosphere.

"Lynda," she said in the hall of the villa, "I'm not staying here long. I want to get back to our own villa and —"

"But you must stay and have some tea first," objected Lynda. "Actually, I've taught this housekeeper woman to make tea in our own English way. Besides, I want to hear all your news. When did Duncan arrive wherever it was you were? Did you know he was going to join you?"

Rianna saw at once how dangerous Lynda's prattling could be. "Oh, it was quite a surprise to me when Duncan came to Trapani. I thought he was still on the yacht." She spoke lightly and casually, for she realised that Martin and Holford had entered the sitting room.

Across the room she met Holford's steely gaze.

"Did you find Trapani interesting?" he asked coldly.

"Yes. In spite of the fact that it's farther north than Marsala and even has a promenade called the North Wind, I found its atmosphere very congenial." She spoke defiantly for the benefit of Holford and he could make what he liked of her remark.

Martin asked about the films she had made and she was inwardly grateful for his help in smoothing an awkward patch.

When Lynda poured tea, Rianna was stabbed by pangs of jealousy, for she saw how easily Lynda had fitted into the household of the Villa Aurelia as its mistress.

Holford stayed only the barest minimum time in which he could swallow a cup of tea. Then he excused himself and went out of the room.

"Is there something wrong?" queried Rianna of her brother in a quiet tone.

Martin sighed. "Holford is in a devil of a temper. Oh, not with you, but Duncan. We were scheduled to go out on the yacht and start diving again today, but without Duncan the programme had to be altered."

"I see," murmured Rianna thoughtfully. "But did Duncan know of the arrangement?"

"I don't know. Holford expected him back here last night from wherever he was and he didn't show up."

Lynda broke in rapidly. "Oh, take no notice. Holford becomes grumpy sometimes, but he gets over it. Men always make such a fuss if trivial little things go wrong."

Rianna knew that postponing a dive was no trivial little thing to Holford.

Martin rose. "I'll leave you two girls to your chat. I've a spot of work to do."

Rianna would have been glad for her brother to stay and relieve her of the necessity of listening to Lynda's "chat", but for the moment there was no alternative.

"Doesn't Duncan get any tea?" she asked airily. "Or has he been sent to his room for bad behaviour?"

Martin laughed. "He's probably getting a dressing-down from the boss. I'll see you later. I'll come back to the Casa Rosa with you when you're ready."

When the two girls were alone Lynda wriggled in her corner of the settee and leaned towards Rianna. "Now, darling, you can tell me everything. Don't be shy. We've got rid of the men for a few minutes."

Rianna stared rather distastefully at the other girl. "What are you expecting me to tell? It was only yesterday that Duncan arrived in Trapani."

"Oh, no. He went tearing off the night before, without saying where he was going."

"But I didn't see him until yesterday morning. So we went to Segesta together and came home today. That's all there is."

Lynda smiled slyly and her eyes danced with amusement.

"That's all – so you say. But you do realise, don't you, that you've made a great hit with Duncan. He can't talk of anyone else."

"I'm sorry about that. He'll soon find other topics of conversation, no doubt."

"Not while you're here in Marsala," prophesied Lynda.

"And how did you enjoy your stay with Emilia's family?" queried Rianna, directing the conversation into an opposing channel.

"Well, it was good – and bad. Their villa is the most sumptuous place; it stands on a hill overlooking the sea and has the most gorgeous grounds full of flowers and trees and statues and the most romantic little nooks for sitting there by moonlight. Then the bedroom I was given –"

"Oh, you stayed several days?"

"Yes. I was invited to stay as long as I liked, but of course I knew when Holford was returning and I did so want to be at home here to welcome him."

Martin, of course, had not known that Lynda was to stay more than a single day at the Cavallinis', but now Rianna was pierced afresh by Lynda's assumption of the right to be chatelaine of Holford's villa.

"You were telling me about your bedroom," she said almost sharply, for Lynda had lapsed into thought, no doubt dwelling on the cordial welcome she had given to Holford a night or two ago, thought Rianna bitterly.

"Oh, yes. That was the most palatial I've ever slept in. All white and gold and a bed with gilded cherubs at the head. Emilia's family must be enormously rich. She has a brother and a cousin and several other young men came in either to dinner or paying afternoon calls." Lynda sighed. "But I didn't see Enrico."

"Oh, the young man you danced with at the hotel. He wasn't there?"

"No. Not rich enough, I should guess. That family wouldn't encourage a poor man to match up with Emilia. She can have her pick of millionaires."

Rianna rose to go. "I must see if Duncan is ready to take Martin and me home."

"Yes, of course. Tell me, Rianna, what sort of lover is Duncan?"

Rianna stared at her companion with horror. "I wouldn't know, Lynda. I've no experience of his lovemaking."

Lynda's mouth opened in a rounded "O". "How surprising! It isn't like him to miss a chance, especially when he so obviously wanted to chase you up – even at the expense of getting himself into trouble with Holford."

For a moment or two Rianna had no answer ready and she saw the gleam of triumph on Lynda's dainty features, the set of her mouth with a half smile that indicated a good scoring point.

Rianna mustered a gracious smile. "You obviously know much more of Duncan's character than I do. He's only a recent acquaintance of mine. But where their business affairs are concerned, I think we'd better leave him and Holford to sort out any misunderstandings. Goodbye, Lynda."

She moved out of the room into the hall, her head held high, aware that she had not been at her most tactful and might have made an enemy of Lynda. But that must be the end to Lynda's sly insinuations.

In the next few minutes Rianna found that it was not the end, but merely the beginning to a tangle of misunderstandings and accusations.

Martin was out in the courtyard and came towards her. "Holford wants me to stay here for an hour or so. I have to give Duncan some details of our next dive. Holford will drive you to the

Casa Rosa."

Rianna drew in her breath with a slight gasp. She was not anxious to meet Holford in his present bad-tempered state, but apparently there was no choice.

"But all my gear – cameras, films, my clothes – are in Duncan's car," she pointed out.

Martin shook his head. "No. They've all been packed into Holford's. Here he comes. I'll be off." He dropped his voice to a whisper. "Any comforting message for Duncan? I'll do what I can to soothe him, but I expect he'd rather have his hand held by you."

Rianna laughed. There was no point in taking offence at a brother's mischievous jibes.

"Are you ready?" Holford was opening the door of his car.

"Quite ready," she answered, but asked herself – ready for what? Surprisingly, during the first part of the drive home he asked only polite questions about the sights of Trapani and Erice.

"Did you look at the coloured bags and carpets at Erice?" he asked.

"Yes. I bought an embroidered runner and I took some close-up photographs of one or two carpets. I wasn't sure if they were actually made by local people in their homes or whether they had small factories there."

"Both, I think. A few of the inhabitants still manage 'cottage' industries, but the rest are made in commercial workshops."

He stopped the car suddenly and she noticed that he had driven some distance along the shore well past the street where the Casa Rosa was situated.

He leaned forward on the wheel and gazed through the windscreen. "Rianna, I have to talk to you," he said, after a long pause.

"Yes?" Her tone was non-committal and certainly not encouraging. She was in no mood to make matters easy for him. If she was to be scolded for her part in Duncan's failure to be at the right place at the right time, then Holford must initiate the homily.

"I know that you're here to do certain work for yourself – and to be with your brother – but we in the diving team also have our schedules and programmes and I'd be obliged if you wouldn't – er – encourage Duncan, or indeed any of the others – to – er –"

"Say it, Holford. Say 'Waste their time with me!' Possibly you should have made it clear to Duncan exactly when he was expected back on the yacht. I assure you I had no hand in either inviting him to Trapani or keeping him there past his due date for return." She had purposely kept her voice calm and without the indignation she felt welling up inside her.

But her very calmness seemed to have the reverse effect on him, for he turned towards her and there was anger in every line of his face. His eyes seemed to flash blue fire.

"I'm not accusing you of any active approach," he snapped. "Duncan has a roving eye for girls and he could hardly resist following you when he knew you were in Trapani."

"And what do you suggest I should have done to prevent him? Send him a note saying 'Please don't follow'? I don't think I'm really quite so arrogant,"

She chose the word deliberately, hoping that he would also apply it to himself.

He continued to stare moodily through the windscreen and she noticed that his mouth was set in sombre lines as though his inner vision was watching something distasteful.

"I'm sure you must know that our work as a team is very important. We're all dependent on each other and for this reason I try my utmost to ensure that none of us have serious outside worries or anxieties." His voice was now smoother and calmer as though he were talking to a young and rather brainless girl.

"Of course I understand that quite clearly," she answered sharply. "My brother is involved with you all and naturally I'm concerned as much for his well-being as for any of the rest of you. But please don't blame me for upsetting time-tables. In future, I'll keep my plans for visits to various parts of the island a dead secret."

She, too, was staring straight ahead. Then when she turned towards Holford, she saw the corners of his mouth lift in a smile. Suddenly he put his hand over hers and even in the midst of her indignation at his unjust accusations, she felt a surge of pleasure at his touch.

"Please forgive me," he said, and when he turned his face towards her, she wished almost that he had continued to stare in some other direction, for the light in his blue eyes confused her, weakening her resolution to vindicate herself of blame.

"I can see that you're not easily trodden down and I'm glad of it," he said quietly. "Martin is lucky to have you for a sister. The truth is that I've extra responsibilities at the moment – unlooked-for problems."

"The arrival of Lynda?" she hazarded mildly, and was unprepared for his violent reaction. He withdrew his hand, started the car and muttered fiercely, "We'll leave Lynda out of our discussions. She's come here because she needs help – and probably I'm the one person who can give her the – the right kind of help."

Rianna was too dumbfounded to reply with an apology or any other form of words. In silence he drove her to the Casa Rosa, unloaded her suitcase and cameras and other parcels from the car and helped her to deposit them in her own courtyard.

"Thank you for bringing all my stuff home," she said, and heard her voice to be thin and uncertain in pitch.

"No trouble," he answered brusquely, walked back to his car and drove off with only the merest hint of a farewell wave.

Rianna stood in the living room of the little house, reviling herself for her clumsiness in mentioning Lynda. Holford could scold her just as he pleased, but the subject of Lynda was evidently taboo. At first, she had been disinclined to believe everything that Duncan had told her about the relationship of Holford and Lynda, but now? It was becoming more obvious that Lynda had some secret hold over Holford and had now come to Sicily to claim what she considered her rights.

Martin came home shortly after her return. "And what was the trip to Trapani really like?" he asked. "I haven't had a chance to find out."

"If you'd asked me an hour ago, I should have said it was

quite satisfactory. Now, after being dragged through the hoop by Holford, I'm not so sure."

Martin laughed easily. "Oh, take no notice of him! He gets rather tetchy over us lot – his team, I mean. Thinks he has to make sure we're not only physically fit, but sound in mind, too. No worries, no problems."

"Then perhaps it's a case of 'Physician, heal thyself.' He may be the tetchiest one," she retorted. "Do you know what's biting him? Is it the arrival of Lynda?"

Martin shrugged. "How should I know? She's obviously the clinging type, so if she finds she can cling to Holford, that's his problem."

Rianna found a grain of comfort in the fact that apparently Martin was not particularly attracted to Lynda.

"I'll take your films and process them for you on the yacht as soon as I can."

"What?" Rianna roused herself from her uncomfortable thoughts. "Oh, yes, that would be a good idea."

After a few minutes she suggested, "Shall we eat in the *pensione* – or somewhere else, if you like? I don't feel I want to bother with preparing a meal here."

They chose the *trattoria* to which Jeffrey, the biologist of the team, had introduced her.

"I'm glad you came home tonight," she said to her brother across the red check tablecloth when they were halfway through the meal.

He grinned. "Lonely without Duncan?"

She was now able to laugh in return. "Not likely. But now that Holford has installed his team at his villa, and you have to spend more time here, it makes me feel more than ever that I'm the odd one out."

The grin had disappeared from Martin's face. "You *have* let Holford's scolding depress you, haven't you? Cheer up! After all, you did know before we came that when I was roaming about in the depths of the ocean, I'd be unable to tour around Sicily with you."

"Yes, of course I guessed that there would be times when I'd have to amuse myself. All the same, quite candidly, I thought we'd all be working together on the yacht. I imagined it would be a larger vessel."

Martin picked up a spare fork and lightly rapped her on the knuckles. "You staying aboard all the time! One girl among half a dozen men – and without a chaperone? Come, come, my dear sister, where are your morals?"

She laughed. "Yes, I suppose we didn't think about it carefully."

"You're not regretting we came?" he asked, a trifle anxiously.

"Indeed, no! When I get a shade more used to the rules and regulations, I'm going to have the time of my life here." Certainly she could feel no regret at having met Holford, even though she was forced to fight against the overpowering longing for him. As for the time of her life, if luck were on her side, this Sicilian venture could indeed be one of the peaks of dramatic intensity to look back on in one's ripe old age.

"We're going to explore some grottoes tomorrow," Martin informed her later in the evening. "Only just up the coast and Holford said something about having dinner aboard the next night and a film show of some of the stuff I've taken."

"That's fine. I hope everything goes well and your films are a success."

Martin's face now wore a slightly mischievous expression. "I've news for you, too. The ladies are invited. You and Lynda, that is."

"Oh, indeed. Holford said nothing about this."

"Perhaps you were so busy giving him your own brand of backchat that such thoughts went out of his mind."

Rianna smiled. She was already deciding not to be present at this "admiral's flagship" party, but discretion prompted her not to sulk in case Martin's chances were damaged. All the same, she needed more confirmation of the affair than a casual mention from her brother.

The following day she received by hand a note from Holford, and his written words delighted her.

". . . hope you will join us on board the *Celestina* tomorrow when we return from our dive.

We'll send the dinghy for you about eight o'clock at the harbour steps. Holford."

There was nothing in those brief sentences to stir her emotions, yet she could not avoid a sense of elation that refused to be subdued.

She schooled herself to work during the two days on her notes of Trapani and Segesta, typing articles and commentaries, but a part of her mind had already winged its way ahead in imagination to this unlooked-for occasion.

She inspected her fairly limited wardrobe and chose a long skirt of beech-leaf brown velvet teamed with a gold lamé blouse. In a shop in Marsala she had purchased an inexpensive pair of chandelier ear-rings of amber glass with delicate gilt trimmings and she decided this was the night to wear them.

With a lacy shawl over her arm she walked the few steps along the street to the main road where she would pick up a taxi.

At the harbour steps there was no sign of a dinghy and at first she could not see the yacht, but after a few minutes a shout alerted her and she saw Martin was waiting with the dinghy.

"Hiya!" he called. "My, my! Is it really my very own sister who's dazzling my old eyes? Smart get-up!" he commented.

"Suitable, I hope, for the admiral's flagship?"

His laughter echoed over the quiet waters of the harbour.

"I can see quite plainly that Duncan, poor fish, has no chance at all," he murmured as he cast off.

Lynda was already aboard and sitting with Holford and Duncan at a small table on deck. The men rose immediately to greet Rianna, pulling a chair for her and asking what she would like to drink.

"Did the diving go well?" she asked Holford presently in a lull in the conversation.

"Excellently. Now that we've all done our proper quota of preliminary exercises, I think we shall soon be able to sail off on a longer expedition."

"I won't ask your destination, because I know you like to keep it secret," said Rianna with a smile.

"Not this time. We shall probably go along the south coast of the island and round to Syracuse."

"Searching for lost ships or wrecks?"

Holford smiled. "Wrecks are incidental, really. If we came across an important find, that would be all to the good, but our main purpose is geological. The land structure is fantastically varied, with Etna dominating and Stromboli permanently blowing its top, so the sea bed and sometimes the cliffs below the usual waterline must also be just as interesting."

"What a pretty outfit you're wearing!" Lynda leaned across Holford to compliment Rianna. Although Duncan was on the other side of Lynda, it was now obvious to Rianna that conversation had gone on long enough between Holford and herself for Lynda to decide to interrupt.

"Thank you," murmured Rianna, and was about to add a mildly insincere compliment in exchange on Lynda's dress, a pale primrose chiffon with flowing knife-pleated sleeves. In the twilight the colour had vanished, leaving Lynda more like a pale moth against the darkening sea.

But a sudden babble of voices halted Rianna's words and a moment later Emilia appeared on deck, followed by Steve, the medical member of the diving team.

On the occasions when Rianna had met Emilia, the Italian girl had seemed extremely composed and serene, but tonight she was bubbling with gaiety.

"If I am late, it is because I had to wait until the darkness was almost here," she explained as someone vacated a chair for her. "Then I slipped away and into the taxi my maid had ordered. So I was glad to be met by Steve at the harbour."

Rianna was slightly mystified by the air of conspiracy and it was only later that she understood Emilia's difficulty in evading her family and succeeding in joining a party of people aboard a yacht in the harbour.

"That girl is hedged round with restrictions," Duncan explained as they were sitting at dinner in the saloon. "Most Italian

91

girls are breaking out of the strict seclusion that's been the custom for centuries, but in Sicily, apparently, you mustn't move without your chaperone."

"But when I've met her before in the hotel, she was surrounded by young men," said Rianna quietly.

Duncan smiled. "That's what you thought, but probably only a few yards away, her duenna was sitting quietly watchful and sharp-eyed."

Now Emilia was reminding the company that tonight she was supposed to be dining with her cousin and his wife at their house in a suburb of Marsala.

"So of course," she explained, her dark eyes sparkling, "I am wearing a dress not suitable for walking about on ships."

Rianna thought Emilia's dress a triumph of material and cut. Heavy dark rose-coloured brocade with a draped bodice cut low at the neck and a fairly narrow skirt that yet seemed to flow; a neckline of finely carved pink tourmalines, a bracelet or two and ear-rings that flashed fire with every movement of Emilia's head.

Jeffrey had prepared a dinner that was easy to serve, for some of the dishes were cold – medallions of lobster in a creamy sauce, followed by rice balls filled with minced meat and tomatoes. The one hot dish was of stuffed chicken served with aubergines and there were several sweets or cheeses to choose to finish.

"You must have spent all day cooking," remarked Rianna, as she helped him to clear the plates and dishes.

"Only part of it," he answered. "Some of the stuff was made yesterday and shoved in the fridge."

Some of the rest of the party had already gone up on deck when Rianna followed. Halfway up the stairs she paused, for Lynda's voice came clearly. "What with Emilia dressed up for a ball and Rianna looking as though she were going to a gypsy's wedding, I felt quite eclipsed."

A man's voice spoke in low tones, no doubt reassuring Lynda that she looked a dream and outshone all other women. Whose voice? Holford's? Rianna waited a few seconds while the sound of Lynda's querulous complaints became more distant, but when she emerged on deck, she saw Lynda escorted by Duncan and they were coming towards her.

"Oh, there you are, Rianna!" exclaimed Lynda. "How sweet of you to help Jeffrey with the washing-up!"

"But I –" began Rianna, disclaiming such comradely assistance, but Lynda interrupted with, "I'm sure you could do with a change of partner, so I'll leave you and Duncan to have a quiet chat together."

She moved along the yacht's rail and disappeared into the shadows cast by the deckhouse.

Rianna and Duncan stood looking at each other, then they both began to laugh. Duncan seized her hand. "Come, my sweet, let's find somewhere to sit and have this quiet chat that Lynda thinks you've earned."

There were two chairs in the stern. Canvas canopies provided relief from unwelcome draughts and Rianna saw no harm in spending a few minutes with Duncan before the film show was ready.

"Could it be that Lynda was anxious to find herself a change of partner?" she queried softly as they sat down.

Duncan finished lighting his cigar. "Well, I suppose I could be counted a very poor substitute for someone more attractive. Actually, she's livid because she imagined she was to be the sole lady guest this evening. I think she can manage to put up with you around, but Emilia – that was the last straw."

"But why? Even now there are only three girls to five men. No one should complain at having a call on one and two thirds of the masculine company."

Duncan clamped a hand on her shoulder. "Dear Rianna, your ideas of a share-out are totally different from Lynda's. All she wants is to break up any tête-à-tête between Holford and Emilia."

"How do you know that one is taking place?"

"I don't, but I think Holford might just possibly seize the small opportunities when they come his way."

Rianna was unsure of his precise meaning and she made no comment, but Duncan's next words fell like lead on her consciousness.

93

"He'd been getting along very nicely with the luscious Emilia since he first came to Marsala and made the acquaintance of her family. Then of course Lynda has to come along to spoil everything for him."

"To spoil?" she echoed faintly. "You mean he was falling in love with Emilia?"

"Undoubtedly. Oh, he was doing his best not to get too involved before the end of the summer. And of course, she's surrounded by plenty of other admirers, most of whom are far more wealthy than Holford. Not that he's particularly poor, but he doesn't reach the rich standards in which Emilia has been brought up."

"One way and another, he seems to be surrounded by problems," she murmured. "I understood that he liked his team to be free from most emotional or psychological tangles."

"So he does, and until now he's been able to steer a very clear course for himself. No entanglements, no responsibilities."

Rianna was about to ask Duncan the exact nature of Holford's responsibility to Lynda, but then Steve came along the deck to say that Martin was ready to project the recent films he had taken.

To make room for the projection equipment, the company on board had to pack themselves into a small space at one end of the saloon and Rianna found herself next to Martin, with Holford on her left hand. Lynda had secured the place on the other side of Holford and made great play of snuggling herself close to him so as to give Jeffrey a good view. Emilia and the other two men were on the opposite side of Martin.

"I'm glad you were able to come tonight," said Holford quietly to Rianna. "You'll be able to see for yourself some of the results of our work, even if you can't take part in it."

"I've seen plenty of Martin's films, but never any of the underwater ones," she answered.

During the next hour or more she was absorbed in the entrancing world below sea-level, yet even as she revelled in the intricacies of colour and light, watched the shoals of fish through which the men moved, she was acutely aware of Hol-

94

ford's magnetic presence close beside her. At one point Martin, who was adding a rough commentary as he went along, mentioned sea-urchins and some kind of jellyfish which could give painful stings to unwary divers.

"The more gorgeous the sea-urchins are in colour, like this red one, the worse jab they can give you with their spines. Like an electric shock."

At that moment, almost as though he had foreseen the effect, Holford grasped Rianna's wrist and she experienced an astonishing electric thrill.

"Naturally, if we're wearing protective suits, we don't feel these pricks," Martin continued, more for the benefit of the women than his companions who already knew such facts.

Rianna thought that she would need a steel-plated armour if she were not to feel the pricks that Holford could cause her merely by touching her at an unexpected moment.

Now she concentrated her attention on the film, watching the sinuous movements of Holford and Duncan as they glided through a blue and green world, pausing to peer into grottoes or effortlessly turn somersaults with no respect for the laws of gravity.

"Switch on the lights, Jeffrey, please," came Martin's voice at the end of that film, "while I change over."

Holford's hand was still lightly clasped over Rianna's wrist and suddenly she became aware of Lynda's hostile gaze.

"Evidently Holford imagines he's in the back row at the cinema, holding the hand of the girl next to him," she said spitefully, but Rianna had already withdrawn her arm away from Holford.

Emilia turned towards him with a radiant smile. "When you are on land, you must be warm and affectionate, to make up for all those hours spent in the cold sea. Perhaps our Mediterranean oceans will have a good effect on all the cold Englishmen and they will become more like Latins."

"So it's the warm seas that make the difference?" queried Duncan. "Then we shall all have to spend more time than ever down among the coral and sea-urchins!"

Rianna blessed these two for giving her time to recover from Lynda's jibe. Holford remained silent, his expression impassive as he watched Martin arranging the spools.

Rianna was startled to see that the new film was one of her own, the shots she had taken in Marsala on that day when Holford had accompanied her. These were followed by scenes of the countryside on her way to Trapani, a fine shot of Giovanni, the man with the donkey, and then the mansions in Trapani and finally the views of the Greek temple at Segesta and the arena theatre.

At the moment she was reasonably satisfied with the results of her first expedition in the island. When the film was finished, Holford asked, "Who was the lone figure on the steps of the Greek theatre at Segesta?"

Before she could reply, Duncan broke in, "I'm surprised you couldn't recognise my handsome profile."

"I was wondering who was the man with the donkey on the country road," remarked Lynda. "How easily you collect men!"

"He was somebody I met along the road," answered Rianna tersely. "In my kind of work, you tend to use people as part of the scenery, to give it life."

"You made a very good film, Rianna." Holford's voice cut decisively across the mild chatter. "If all your work comes up to that standard, you have a most assured future before you." His sincere compliment warmed her and she felt her cheeks flushing with pride. But his next words came near to leading to disaster.

"I shall have to think seriously about taking you on as a camerawoman, as assistant to Martin. But you'll have to learn to dive first."

Rianna knew his words were not intended to be taken seriously, but before she could frame an innocuous answer, Lynda rushed in with a warning, "Don't let him persuade you, Rianna! He's very unlucky with his cameramen. Goodness only knows what would happen if he had to be responsible for girls splashing about in the sea."

Several pairs of eyes were now fixed accusingly on Lynda's

unperturbed face. There was a heavy, if brief, silence. Then Steve rose, saying, "Let's have a drink. Martin deserves one anyway."

The diversion was welcomed and in the general shuffling of chairs being moved, Rianna spoke to her brother. "Thank you for doing my film. I didn't know you'd had time yet."

"I thought you might like – people – to see it."

She knew that by "people" he meant Holford and she was grateful. She slipped out of the door and went quickly up to the deck. Sooner or later Martin would ask her the meaning of Lynda's malicious remark about Holford's bad luck with his cameramen – unless someone had already told him about Jack Patterson.

She leaned against the taffrail, savouring the sheer joy of idling on a yacht in a Mediterranean harbour. The town of Marsala was bathed in a glow of light, fading to pin points on the outskirts along the coast. In the harbour the masthead lanterns of a dozen boats of varying sizes were reflected in restless ripples of water crossing each other to make a fantastic pattern.

After the warmth of the saloon below, Rianna was glad of these few minutes alone in the cooler air. When she heard footsteps approaching, she guessed they would belong to Duncan, but it was Holford's voice that said, "I wondered where you'd gone."

"Did you think I'd fallen overboard?" she queried lightly.

"If you had I'm sure there would have been no lack of gallant rescuers."

"Yes, probably – if anyone had seen me slip over the side in the darkness. Supposing –?"

"Stop such gloomy conjectures," he interrupted. "Surely you wouldn't want to spoil such a charming outfit as the one you're wearing." He fingered the gold lamé blouse and his touch on her shoulder was like fire that sent throbbing pulses down her arm.

She had the presence of mind to move an inch or two away from him.

"That film you made of Segesta –" he began, and she was infinitely glad that he had veered off on another tack. She waited

97

for him to continue. "Some of those shots were first-class. In several you had the temple appearing to float between earth and sky and that's exactly the way it appears from some angles. You must have taken great pains to get that effect."

"I was most impressed by the contrast of golden stone against the blue sky. The whole place gave me a feeling of poetry. When you walk in the bare interior between the massive columns, you know you're treading where many others trod in that same space twenty-five centuries ago." She paused, wondering if her tongue was running away with her.

"I share that feeling. When so much of the world is being steadily destroyed and monstrosities erected, it's good to make acquaintance with some elegant ruins and hope they will stand there for another few centuries. In the water when we dive, I find this idea of antiquity even stronger, for often we're exploring a world that was once dry and is now covered by sea and it all happened millions of years ago, not just thirty or forty centuries."

"Some of that I could grasp from seeing Martin's films tonight," she said. "Lately he's been reading a number of books about underwater geology and I've seen the photographs showing the strata."

"In a volcanic island like Sicily, you never know what evidence you may find that indicates the changes that took place in the earth structure."

"You can't see Etna from here, apparently," she said when he paused.

"You can from a little way inland, but you'll have a closer view of it when we go round the coast to Syracuse. I've told Martin of our plans to take the *Celestina* there and possibly you could join us."

"Not on the yacht?"

His hands grasped her shoulders and he laughed. "You know perfectly well that we've no room for you aboard. No, I meant you could come overland, stopping to do your own exploring wherever you fancied."

She became aware that from somewhere at the other end of the yacht came the sound of singing – or perhaps it was on another boat in the harbour. Men's voices, lightened, then pierced by a high clear soprano.

Held so close to Holford, she was in a turmoil, afraid to melt into his arms and equally reluctant to pull even an inch away.

"What are they singing?" she asked, hardly caring who were the singers or what kind the song.

"Sicilian songs," he whispered. "Sicilian love songs! Entirely suitable for a night like this."

His lips caressed her mouth gently, then more fiercely, and she gave herself to his embrace, responding as she had never dreamed possible with any man. Then although he retained his grasp of her elbows, he pushed her away from him.

"Forgive me, Rianna. That was quite unpardonable. I don't know – put it down to the night – and the music – and Sicily."

She wanted to say that from her point of view there was nothing to forgive, but he took her roughly by the arm and marched her along the deck.

"We'd better join the others."

Her heart felt like a stone. Yes, join the others, so that he should not be tempted into any more disgraceful scenes like kissing Rianna.

The rest of the party were grouped around Emilia, who was now singing solos. Light from two lanterns at either end of a wide canopy flickered and slanted on the faces of the group. As Rianna slid unobtrusively into a vacant chair, she saw Lynda's face, questioning, hostile, disconsolate, all at the same time.

When Emilia's unaccompanied song ended, she was rewarded by a burst of clapping and murmured "Encores". Then from an adjacent boat came the sound of a mandolin playing a melody that was joyful and lilting, yet held an undertone of sadness. A voice from across the water invited another song and after some initial hesitation, Emilia picked up the air, one obviously that she knew well, and her beautiful voice floated over the dark waters.

This time at the end of her song, there was a long silence and then only subdued applause from those aboard the *Celestina* and the unseen audience on other boats.

"Enough!" declared Emilia, in response to the "Encores". "My voice does not care for the night air, especially on the sea."

It was time to go ashore. The three girls stepped into the dinghy with Martin and Duncan. Holford had disappeared, but Steve and Jeffrey remained aboard to wait for the dinghy to return to take them off the yacht.

Emilia insisted that she must take a taxi alone, without escort. "You understand that I have been dining at my cousin's, so naturally, I would return home alone." She gave a mischievous trill of laughter as she waved when her taxi drew away.

Martin and Rianna allowed Lynda and Duncan to take the next taxi that came along, but it was obvious that Lynda was hardly delighted to have Duncan for her escort.

When eventually Martin found another taxi, he sat in the corner and remained remarkably silent for him. At last he said, "Lovely voice – Emilia's, I mean."

"Yes. She could easily become a professional singer."

Martin gave a grunt. "Her family would never allow that. Look at the way she had to slip out tonight to come aboard the yacht. There are quite a lot of things her family won't allow – and tying herself up with an insignificant Englishman is one of them."

At first, in her half-dreamy state of inattention, Rianna thought he was referring to Holford, who could never be dismissed as "insignificant", but almost immediately she realised with a shock that her brother was becoming deeply attached to Emilia. She hoped that his affection would eventually be no more than a passing admiration. In her own mind there was this haunting dread that she now had two rivals where Holford was concerned – Lynda, who was striving to re-establish a former claim, and Emilia, to whom he had evidently been attracted before Lynda's sudden appearance in Sicily.

"Emilia is so strikingly beautiful that every man falls in love with her," murmured Rianna.

"But it isn't only her beauty," protested Martin. "She's warm and witty and kind." Then he laughed more lightly. "She com-

100

pletely puts Lynda in the shade, doesn't she? Makes her look wishy-washy."

Rianna remembered those overheard remarks. "I expect she thinks Emilia was dressed for a ball – and I was decked up for a gypsy's wedding."

"Well, you both looked rather more vital than Lynda tonight."

In the sitting room of the Casa Rosa, just as Rianna was saying goodnight to her brother, he exclaimed suddenly, "Do you know you've only one ear-ring on? Lost the other?"

She put up her hand and tugged at her ear-lobe. "M'm. It must have dropped off somewhere."

He put an affectionate arm around her waist. "Don't tell me it came off in a desperate clinch. You and Holford were missing for quite some time after the film show. Lynda remarked on it to Duncan."

Rianna disengaged herself from her brother's clasp. "Lynda remarks on everything – if it remotely concerns Holford."

"Yes, I suppose she wouldn't have landed herself on him unless she's convinced he's going to marry her."

Unwittingly, even Martin was now stabbing Rianna afresh, but she must not let him know.

Rianna took refuge in a loud yawn. "I'm tired. I need some sleep."

Yet in bed sleep was elusive. She could not decide whether Holford was a man who distributed his favours as evenly as possible so that no woman should know of his exact intentions until he chose to reveal them, or whether between his desire for Emilia and Lynda's ruthless pursuit, he found solace in a cosy half-hour with Rianna. Perhaps he imagined that she was on the fringe of events and there would be no complications. If so, then she felt cheapened.

In the darkness, she laughed quietly. If Holford could only see inside her mind!

CHAPTER SIX

RIANNA spent the next two days working on her articles and travel notes, as well as filling out some of Martin's rough headings for the films he had taken. She was also planning a trip along the southern coast of Sicily to Selinunte and Agrigento and refused to listen to an inner voice that whispered – "You're planning to go that way because you know the yacht – and Holford – are heading for Syracuse."

I have to do my work in the order I find most convenient, she told herself sharply.

When Martin came in one lunch-time, he said, "Holford wants to know if it's all right for you to visit the wine-vaults – Emilia's family business."

"When?" she queried.

"Tomorrow."

"M'm. I'd intended to start for Agrigento tomorrow." Not even to Martin was she prepared to give the impression that she was eager to rush into the proposition. "I suppose I could start a day or two later. What am I supposed to do? Present myself at the office door?"

Martin shrugged. "I wouldn't know that, but evidently arrangements have been made for you."

When she did not speak for a few moments, he added, "No doubt you could postpone the visit until the date fits in better."

"No, I'll go tomorrow," she decided. "When does Holford intend to start on his next trip to Syracuse?"

"Not for several days, I gather. So, as long as I do my daily quota of swimming and running and other exercises, I'm free as a bird." After a pause he added, "I suppose there wouldn't be any point in my coming to the wine-cellars with you?"

"If you can spare the time, why not?"

He turned away. "No. I don't suppose Emilia would be there. It's not quite her cup of tea – or glass of Marsala – escorting visitors around her father's business."

Rianna laughed. "If I should see her, I'll tell her what you said – that she's a lazy drone and bone idle. Just a girl for pleasure."

"That's nothing to what I could tell Holford about you. Or even Duncan, for that matter!" he threatened.

"Well, let's forget these revelations. What am I to do about tomorrow? Let Holford know – or telephone the wine place?"

"Have a word with Holford, I should think. He's probably at the Villa Aurelia."

When Rianna telephoned later, it was Lynda who answered.

"You want to speak to Holford? He's not here at this moment. Can I give him a message?"

Rianna hesitated. She certainly did not want to discuss the matter with Lynda. After a pause, she said, "Will you tell him it will be all right for tomorrow?"

Lynda gave a little trill of laughter. "Oh, really! What are you up to? Is it a secret rendezvous?"

"Not exactly. Just a business call."

"Ah, but I know how fascinating and exciting some business calls can be. Why are you so mysterious?"

Rianna forced a light laugh. "I didn't know that I was being mysterious. You're the one who's making the mystery."

"Very well, if you don't want to –"

Rianna cut in with, "Look, Lynda, it's a simple visit to a wine-vault. It's part of my work and Holford has merely arranged it with the manager there."

"Oh, I see. Emilia's father's firm. Is Holford going with you?"

"I should imagine that's very unlikely," replied Rianna, dryly.

"Because if he is, I shall ask him to take me, too," said Lynda decisively.

"Why? Are you afraid I might push him into a butt of Marsala?" asked Rianna, feeling that it was now her turn to poke a little harmless fun at Lynda.

"I might be afraid of far worse things than that," retorted Lynda acidly, not relishing the joke at her expense.

"All right," Rianna said reassuringly. "You'll give Holford the message, won't you?"

"Indeed, yes. I'll see that he gets the message."

When she had replaced the receiver in the hall of the adjacent *pensione,* Rianna remained thoughtful for several minutes. That last sentence of Lynda's – "I'll see that he gets the message" – held a darker shade of meaning than the mere fact of conveying news from one person to another. What else could I have done? Rianna asked herself. Telephoned later, making sure that Holford would be there? In that case, Lynda would have been even more suspicious.

Even now, Rianna realised that she had no details of the time she was expected, but could only assume, in the absence of other directions, that about ten o'clock would be appropriate. During the rest of the day and the evening, she half hoped that Holford would ring back to confirm, but no word came from him.

She presented herself next morning at the offices of the Cavallini firm and was surprised and delighted to find Holford waiting for her.

She had not seen him since the night of the party on the *Celestina* and for her part was a little uncertain of what attitude to adopt, but Holford evidently had the knack of putting the immediate past behind him, for he greeted her with the easy assurance of a welcoming friend.

"I wasn't sure of the time I was to come," she said, casting a discreet but searching glance around to discover if Lynda had accompanied him. "But Lynda gave you my message, evidently."

He gave her a disarming grin and the expression in his blue eyes was evasive. "Yes. I was out in the garden. Lynda could have called me to the phone. But you're here, that's the main thing." He led the way through the office to a passage leading to a courtyard. "She wanted to come along with me," he added in a casually careful manner, "but I persuaded her that she

104

wouldn't really be interested and that it would turn out to be a very tiring morning."

Rianna digested this piece of flagrant conspiracy as she accompanied him to a door in a stone wall, where a guide was waiting. It was useless not to feel elated that he had rejected the company of Lynda in favour of Rianna's. Her spirits began to bubble up into a sense of delight, but of course she would have more sense than to let him see that she was inwardly dancing with joy.

He introduced her to the foreman who was to conduct them over the establishment and explain the various processes. "Signor Casoni is the man who makes all the decisions about the wine," explained Holford. "He has worked for the Cavallinis all his life, so he knows by now how Marsala should be made."

Rianna now saw that part of the vaults were situated in what remained of an old monastery with cloisters.

"Very handy for storage of casks," remarked Holford.

Signor Casoni's English was adequate enough for Rianna to comprehend most of his explanations, but when he failed, Holford translated for her benefit.

"You understand, *signorina,* that this is not the time of year for the grape harvest to arrive with us," the foreman told her. "That must wait until September or October."

"What kind of grapes go into Marsala?" Rianna asked.

"Our local grapes from Trapani and Marsala provinces. First we use a dry white wine made from them. Then we mix brandy with *passito* wine – that is, wine made from slightly dried grapes."

"To raise the alcohol content?" queried Holford.

"Indeed so. Thirdly, we heat very slowly young, unfermented 'must' – you understand that in new wine – until it becomes dark and sweet and almost like caramel."

"Oh, that's what gives Marsala that slightly burnt flavour," commented Rianna.

Signor Casoni nodded. "All these contributions must be rested for a long period, then they are blended together and must rest again."

"For how long?" asked Rianna.

"From the beginning, perhaps we take four years," was the reply. "Then Marsala is ready to drink."

"A rich, walnut brown wine with a delicious aroma,' added Holford. "Both Nelson and Garibaldi knew what to buy for their men!"

The party moved on to another corridor, where Rianna was fascinated by the long lines of wooden casks, the bottom ones resting on a hollowed strip of concrete, the others piled neatly on top. She had brought her two cameras with her, but Holford had already pointed out that there was little need for her to take many photographs, as the firm would provide her with publicity material, photographs and brochures.

"Perhaps that's just as well," she agreed, "for the lighting is not very strong."

"Wine does not care for too much bright light," observed Signor Casoni. "It likes a dim – perhaps religious light."

"And that you certainly have acquired here, with the old cloisters and the monks' former cells with tiny windows."

The foreman took Holford and Rianna to the bottling department, where he displayed several machines at work. "It is not only Marsala wine made here," he explained. "We make several other Sicilian wines for the table."

Presently he announced, "We shall now go to the sampling room where you will be able to taste our wines."

Rianna discovered that there were actually two sampling rooms – one where the wines were tested and tasted at every stage – this was in a darkened room in a corner of the cloister.

"Choose wines – and women – by candlelight," Holford murmured, as Signor Casoni held up a glass of rich reddish-amber against a candle flame.

Rianna glanced quickly at Holford, eager to find in his face perhaps some indication that he was not entirely indifferent to her, but he, too, was holding a glass of wine against the candlelight, tilting it one way and another.

The other sampling or tasting room was close to the business offices and intended for clients to taste the various bottlings and vintages before buying.

106

"Your buyers from England come here to taste the Marsala," Signor Casoni said proudly.

Then the door opened and Emilia came in, her arms full of booklets and brochures.

"I am so very sorry that I seem to have missed you," she said to Rianna and Holford. "I was told wrongly that you were in other parts of our rambling old rabbit-warren. But here, Rianna, are some documents that will help you with your work. You will see there are many good photographs and the text is also in English."

Rianna was almost too stunned to answer, but she collected her wits and thanked Emilia, who was now turning to Holford with a smile. "I hope you have given Rianna a good account of what we do."

"Signor Casoni has already done that," Holford replied, and Rianna found herself jealously watching the smiles that passed between him and Emilia.

"You hold some position here?" queried Rianna, wondering if she had misjudged Emilia who might even work in the place.

"Oh, indeed no!" Emilia shuddered slightly. "Wine vaults are not for me to roam in. I came this morning because Holford asked me to collect what information I could on your behalf while you were in the cellars and save you from making so many notes."

"Thank you very much," Rianna murmured through stiff lips. It was all quite obvious now why Holford had not wanted Lynda to be present. Certainly he had not intended Lynda to know that he was meeting Emilia here, but of course it did not matter if Rianna were suddenly confronted with the Italian girl. Rianna seethed with fury and resentment. She would make her escape at the earliest moment and leave Holford to dally as long as he liked with the lovely Emilia.

Vaguely she heard some mention of lunch and before she could prevent herself, she said curtly, "No, thanks, Holford, I'll go back to my villa."

Then she saw Emilia's surprised expression. "But you must stay. We shall lunch with my father and his manager and they will answer any of your queries."

Docilely, Rianna allowed events to roll over her head and in half an hour she was seated between Signor Cavallini and Holford, lunching in what was obviously the Cavallini private dining-room, a beautiful apartment with handsome frescoes and ornate window embrasures.

She forced herself to be businesslike and keep her mind on the subject of this morning's visit. She asked what she hoped were intelligent questions and stored in her memory the helpful answers she received, but it was after the meal was over that her outward calmness was shattered.

As she was conducted to the store outside which a line of barrels waited for transport to the docks and shipment abroad, Holford walked beside her.

"I've something of yours, Rianna," he said in a quiet voice. He fished in a pocket and pulled out her missing ear-ring, the amber chandelier, which she had lost on the night of the party aboard the *Celestina*.

In other circumstances she would have been delighted at having the trifle returned, but today her nerves were on edge owing to the necessity of maintaining a façade of politeness in front of the Cavallinis.

She had halted and now stared first at the ear-ring lying in the palm of Holford's hand, then at his face with his blue eyes gleaming with a kind of cordial mischief.

"I'd given up hope of seeing it again," she said coldly, resuming walking behind the others. "It's not valuable – just something I bought here in an idle hour."

"Well, take it. It's no use to me."

His words were ill-chosen. She turned towards him. "I can well understand that – unless, of course, you collect similar small trophies from other girls on whom you bestow a casual kiss in the dark."

His expression froze, as though a blind had been drawn down over his face. "What on earth do you mean?" he demanded harshly.

"Only that I'm not willing to –"

"Come along, Rianna!" Emilia's voice prevented any further discussion and Rianna could not decide whether to be glad or sorry that she had not been given time to make a fuller explanation to Holford. Perhaps, she thought, she had said enough to make him realise that she was not a girl who appreciated a casual embrace and a few meaningless kisses.

Now she gave her attention to the scene in front of her. A vine-covered pergola stretched between the roof of the single-storey building and a strip of earth beyond a cobbled roadway.

"As this is early in the year, the vines do not give much shade," explained Signor Cavallini, "but in the summer when the sun is hot, then the leaves are thick, and also in the autumn," he added, with a smile, "we can pick a grape or two as we work."

The barrels were lined up on a raised platform that ran the length of the building and Rianna noticed that it was roughly at the same level as the lorries. One man guided the barrel on to the tailboard of the lorry while two men rolled the barrels into position on the floor of the lorry.

"Doesn't the wine become shaken about and agitated too much with all this movement?" asked Rianna. "On to lorries, then ships and unloaded at the other ports and so on?"

"When the casks arrive, they are rested," she was informed by the manager. "The wine settles down before it is bottled."

"Perhaps I could take one or two photographs of my own?" she suggested. "I would like to have a souvenir of this particular day." She shot a stony glance at Holford.

"That is a most happy thought," replied Emilia warmly, arranging herself between her father and Holford.

Rianna focussed her camera on the group. "That's a formal one," she said. "Now perhaps you would stand about more informally, as though you were just chatting to each other."

Signor Cavallini was happy to oblige and posed himself as though addressing or instructing his manager, while Holford and Emilia were in profile.

"Shall we actually talk to each other?" queried Emilia, laughing.

"Of course!" replied Rianna. "If you can't think of anything
109

else, say the multiplication table. It's an old stage trick."

Rianna took various other shots of the men loading the casks and declared herself well satisfied with all she had seen and been told.

She thanked Emilia and Signor Cavallini for their hospitality and kindness in touring her around. "If I am able to sell my article, I shall of course send you copies."

Rianna returned to the office where she had left all the brochures and booklets that Emilia had given her. All the publicity material had been neatly packed into a cardboard box and it was Holford who took charge of it.

"One of our cars will take you to your villa," offered Emilia, handing Rianna her ciné camera. "And you, Holford? Where is your destination?"

"I'm not quite sure," he said slowly, looking at Rianna as he spoke.

"Then you must tell the chauffeur if you want to go to the harbour for the yacht, or to your villa," Emilia said crisply.

Rianna was now apprehensive about sharing a car-ride with Holford. She knew that he would refer again to the lost earring.

Holford twisted the situation to his own advantage, she thought grimly.

"Yes, I'll go to the harbour, so we'll go there first," he decided.

When he and Rianna reached the point from which he usually took the dinghy out to the *Celestina,* he spoke to the chauffeur, instructing the man to take the box of publicity material to the Casa Rosa.

"The *signorina* and I will get out here and walk. You need not wait for us. Then you can return to the wine offices."

Rianna stared at him in hostile amazement. She had understood the gist of his Italian phrases to the driver. She was in a cleft stick and both she and Holford knew it. She could not make a scene by countermanding the instructions, but, equally, she was in no mood to agree tamely to any suggestion Holford might now make.

"Come, Rianna," he said, as she hesitated to alight from the

110

car. "I'll take you to a café nearby and we'll have coffee or some other drink."

She had no choice but to step out of the car, watch it drive off in the direction of her villa, and then walk beside Holford.

He did not speak for several minutes. Then she broke the silence. "I thought you were going to abduct me aboard the yacht."

He gave her a sharp glance. "Is that what you're aching for?"

"No, indeed. Dry land suits me better at the moment."

"Then don't put ideas into my head or I might not be able to resist such temptation."

Neither spoke again until they had reached a sea-front café. "Coffee or ice-cream?" he asked in his most solicitous manner.

"Coffee, please." She reviled herself for her weakness in sitting down at the same table with him. She should have refused his company, called a taxi and gone home, but she was captive just as much as if she were bound by chains to the chair she sat on.

For a time he spoke of trivial matters, small details concerning the Cavallini wine-making; then he launched into some of Marsala's ancient history – the Carthaginians, the Romans.

"You know that the word 'Marsala' is a corruption of 'Marsa-al-Allah', the Harbour of God?" he queried.

"No, I didn't know. I know its older name was 'Lilybaeum' and also that Garibaldi landed here in –"

"In 1860. He was clever choosing a good flat shore."

All this time Rianna was aware that the conversation was on a superficial level, mere words strung together, while a deeper layer of her mind was occupied with very different matters.

But Holford knew the precise moment when to spring a surprise upon her. Just when she was almost congratulating herself on avoiding the dangerous issues that lay between them, he said, "Are you in the mood to accept your lost ear-ring now?"

She looked away across the promenade to the dark cobalt sea and luminous sunset sky. Let him make the next move, she thought angrily.

When she looked across the table at him, he was dangling the ear-ring over her coffee-cup.

111

"Where did you find it? Or shouldn't I ask that?"

"I ought to tell you that it fell into my pocket and rested against my heart, but the truth is I saw something shining on the deck and picked it up."

"I don't think I want it back," she said slowly. "Perhaps I could give you the fellow-one and you could make a present of the pair to – to some girl of the moment."

He frowned at her and his mischievous good humour had vanished. "What's biting you, Rianna?"

"I don't care much for your attitude. I'm a person in my own right – not just Martin's sister, a girl who happens to be handy on a beautiful night with romantic music in the air."

When she met his gaze, she quailed before the furious light in his eyes. "Perhaps you would have preferred Duncan on that occasion."

She shook her head vehemently. "I came here to work, to help my brother. I wasn't seeking romance."

"I trust then that you won't find it. It would be a pity if anything of that nature disturbed your working schedule."

His sarcasm hurt her almost unbearably and she blinked away the tears that welled up in her eyes, turning her head away so that he should not see how vulnerable she was. Oh, don't let me disgrace myself now, she prayed, and cast a cautious glance around the other tables. But they were empty and only an elderly waiter stood by the door.

Holford stood up to leave, put some coins and notes on the table and nodded to the waiter.

As she accompanied Holford along the harbour wall, she thought drearily that she had now completely wrecked any slender chance she might once have had of any permanent bond between her and this man, arrogant, casually indifferent to the effect his condescending attentions might have on the girls he favoured at the moment. If she had fallen in love with such a man, then the best course was to extricate herself out of such foolish notions as speedily as possible.

Suddenly he stopped at a point where the wall jutted out at an angle near a flight of steps. "What a bad-tempered girl you are!"

he said teasingly.

"I? And what about you? Walking along like a dragon who's furious because his fire-breathing apparatus doesn't work."

He roared with laughter. "And do you cast yourself in the drama as the defenceless maiden? That would be hard to believe. You're too practical for that."

"I don't know which way to take that remark," she retorted. "Compliment or otherwise."

"Then are you the sort of girl who expects compliments, especially if they're flattering?"

"I certainly shouldn't expect them from you."

He pulled a long face mockingly. "Then I've evidently not acquired the art where you're concerned. Perhaps I should remedy that lack."

She longed to say that he need not take the trouble, but remembered that whatever altercations might take place Holford was still Martin's employer.

When she turned her head to meet his gaze, the dancing light in his eyes disconcerted her and she lowered her glance.

"And – for the third time – what shall I do with the ear-ring? Or do you want to set the fashion of wearing only one of a pair?"

"I might do worse than that," she said with spirit. "I'm quite capable of being an individual."

"Right," he answered crisply. "Here goes – and I hope you regret it." He flung up his arm and before she could follow that swift movement the ear-ring described an arc and dropped into the waters of the harbour.

"Now I shall be forced to wear only one," she commented in her smoothest tone, "or else cease to wear any others when I'm in your company."

He leaned easily against the wall, his eyes half closed, his mouth lifted in a slight curve that could hardly be called a smile.

"Are you expected at home at your villa?" he queried. "I suppose Martin won't starve if you're not there to cook his dinner?"

What mischief was he up to now? she wondered. She paused before answering, debating on the wisdom of agreeing to the half-hinted suggestion that he was inviting her to dinner. Must she always yield to whatever line of conduct he wished to pursue when the fancy took him? But the thought now entered her head like a flash that she would be alone with him, that Lynda would not be present – nor possibly even the ravishing Emilia. Yet, in the light of today's events, how could she be sure of that?

"No. Martin can always eat at the *pensione* next door. In fact, he's not too keen on my cooking."

"I began to wonder what murky thoughts you were considering just then. You took so long to reply."

"You must learn not to expect an eager 'Yes' to all your demands," she said severely, surprised to find herself fencing with him.

"I made no demands," he reminded her. "I asked a simple question."

"And was the answer satisfactory?"

"I shall have to wait until much later in the evening before I know that. Come, Rianna, we'll have dinner at a place I know up in the hills – if you're willing, that is," he added with mocking courtesy.

She laughed. "Sooner or later this evening, I shall be hungry. Where is this place in the hills?"

The town of Marsala lay spread on the flat shores of this corner of the island and it was some distance inland before the lower slopes of the hills began.

In the taxi as it wound along a narrow road, Rianna regretted that Holford had given her no opportunity of returning to the villa to freshen up and change her dress, but, crushing down the elation she felt because he was taking her out for the evening apparently on the spur of the moment, this was a small price to pay and perhaps there would be some facility at whatever hotel or inn he had chosen.

The taxi eventually stopped in a small courtyard dimly lit with a couple of lanterns. Then Holford took her arm and led her through a vine-coloured pergola, down some steps, then up another flight until there was light streaming out of what was apparently a rounded building.

114

She glanced upwards and saw the dark silhouette of a tower.

"Oh!" she exclaimed eagerly. "This is the second tower I've visited." She told him about the place where she had lunched in Erice on her trip to Trapani and Segesta.

"Yes, I know the place," he answered. "But this is different."

She realised then that it was likely that he imagined she had been accompanied by Duncan on that occasion, but now, wisely, she remained silent.

Inside the tower was an amazing sight. The ground floor was occupied by a semi-circular bar and the rest of the circumference by serving tables. It appeared that the diners had to climb short flights of wooden stairs to reach platforms where each small table with its attendant chairs jutted out over space, but fortunately had a guard rail around the edges. Thick beams of blackened wood supported the precarious platforms and a continuous boarded space ran round close to the tower walls so that the waiters might have access for serving meals.

"What imagination to design a place like this!" Rianna murmured as she and Holford some time later sat on stools at the bar. She was still wearing the caramel colour trouser suit which she had donned this morning, believing it to be the most suitable outfit for a day at the wine-vaults.

Naturally, she had not expected to be dining out, least of all with Holford, in a romantic tower building that held an aura of medieval grandeur tinged with a slightly sinister atmosphere. But she had been directed to a small annexe equipped with all mod. cons. and had freshened up, renewing her make-up and adding touches of solid perfume to wrists and temples. She was glad of the dim, lantern-lit interior of the tower and hoped that she would pass muster for Holford as his evening partner.

When eventually they climbed the stairs to reach the second tier of tables affixed to the tower walls, and were shown to a table, Rianna laughed. "How fortunate that I don't mind heights or become dizzy!"

Holford looked across at her with a slightly contrite air. "Oh, sorry! I didn't think to ask."

"You just assumed that —"

"That you were exceptionally level-headed," he finished for her.

The food was delicious, although sometimes Rianna was not quite sure what she was eating. She was so blissfully happy that Holford was taking the trouble to entertain her for even one evening that she forgot to ask the names of the various dishes. The dessert stage was reached when an announcement from the ground floor below indicated that a floor show was about to start.

"All this and a floor show, too!" she said, raising her wineglass and moving her chair slightly nearer to the guard rail.

Three jugglers performed incredible balancing feats with spinning plates, bottles and what appeared to be valuable porcelain vases. From this tree-top viewpoint, the foreshortened performers looked like comic dwarfs. Then two musicians played acrobatically on each other's instruments, mandolin and accordion, tumbling over each other in contorted positions, but never losing the rhythm or melody.

Rianna clapped enthusiastically as they finally disentangled themselves. Finally, the spectacle ended with a balancing act of a human pyramid all on the shoulders of one man below while the topmost member threw flowers to the diners in the tiered enclosures.

Holford dexterously caught a carnation, sniffed it first, then twirled it by the stem and handed it to Rianna.

She flushed with pleasure, murmuring a low, sincere, "Thank you."

"Now we must climb to the top of the tower and see the view," he suggested.

She wondered how much of a view they would see in the dark, but out on the roof she caught her breath at the whole panorama stretched out below, the distant glittering mass that was the centre of Marsala with the arms of the harbour thrusting out like tentacles beaded with lights. Away on either side of the town the inky shadows were pinpointed with lights gradually growing fewer until they faded into the velvety darkness.

"Impressive?" queried Holford softly. "Was it worth the climb up here?"

"Oh, yes. Every step." She was intoxicated by his nearness, by the delight of being his privileged partner tonight, but she was careful not to lean too close to him as they peered over the balustrade. There were other couples up here and the fact that one pair was locked in a close embrace must not induce her to suppose that Holford would follow suit.

When they had descended the tower to the ground and came to the garden surrounding it, he apparently took it for granted that she would be willing to stroll through this enchanted paradise for as long as he thought fit or until she complained that her feet ached. He tucked her hand inside his elbow and she adjusted her step to his slow pacing. In companionable silence she walked with him along the paths, adequately illumined where there were steps to negotiate, until they came to a small fountain murmuring into a basin that caught an occasional light and reflected it in broken patterns. Overhead the pines stirred and whispered to each other, occasionally breaking into a sharp creaking as though they were stretching their limbs and groaning with the effort.

She and Holford retraced the way through the garden until they came out by the courtyard where the taxi had deposited them. She remembered that he had paid off the driver and now wondered how the homeward journey would be made. There were no waiting taxis and only two cars parked in the shadows.

Holford turned to smile at her and she saw the planes of his face and the uplifted curve of his mouth as he asked, "Worrying about how we return to Marsala?" She could not see his eyes, but she knew from the tone of his voice that he was mildly baiting her.

"Would you expect me to walk all the way down that road to the town?"

"It's not impossible. It could be done."

"Of course, but I'd prefer to tackle it in daylight."

"And if there's no alternative? What then?" His voice was still teasing.

"I shall beg two of the strongest waiters to give me a bandy-chair."

Now he laughed. "That would be quite a spectacle! But if you'll wait patiently for a few more minutes, I can promise that I have a vehicle coming for us."

Rianna perched herself on the stone coping at the edge of the courtyard. Half a dozen people came presently, laughing and chatting, and piled themselves into the two cars and drove off.

"Good," muttered Holford. "I'm glad they've gone first."

After a few more minutes, Rianna heard the sound of horses' hooves. Expecting a solitary rider, she was surprised when a horse-drawn carriage wheeled into the courtyard.

"Come, Rianna. In you get," ordered Holford. In dumb amazement she obeyed and it was not until the vehicle had left the courtyard and was carefully descending the narrow unlit road that she began to savour the delicious novelty of the ride home.

"What sort of carriage do they call this?" she asked.

"I'm not sure if the Sicilians have their own special name for it, but at home I suppose it might be called a barouche. I think that's the one with a hood at the back. Do you want it pulled up to shut out the draughts?"

"No. I'm not cold and I want to see the countryside as we go." The moon had risen and was now bathing the landscape in silvery light with dense, ink-blue shadows. "Besides," she added, "if we should meet anyone on the road, I shall lean out and bow graciously to them in the manner of royalty."

Holford laughed. "Trust you to give yourself grand airs!"

The road was deserted so far and Rianna seemed unlikely to have the chance to practise her regal gestures on any night-wanderer.

Tiredness was beginning to creep over her. It had been a long day, exciting, irritating, surprising at various times, but always with Holford at the centre of events. Now with the soothing sound of the horse clopping along, presently joined by the driver singing quietly to himself and the night, Rianna counted it as a fairy-tale ending to a romantic evening.

One searing thought flashed across her mind. If Emilia were here, she would undoubtedly join the driver in his Sicilian songs.

But Rianna deliberately shut out such thoughts and unconsciously closed her eyes.

She wakened, aware of a change of rhythm, and realised that she was home, outside her own villa. There was something else to realise, too. Evidently she had fallen asleep and lolled her head on to Holford's shoulder. His arm was around her waist, but now as the horse was pulled up, he released her.

"You're tired," he said softly, as one might say the words to a sleepy child. "You've had a long day."

She was wide awake now, confused and slightly ashamed of having put herself in so vulnerable a position. "But I've enjoyed it. Thank you, Holford."

"Enjoyed all of it?" he queried. "Even when you were ticking me off? Perhaps that was the best part of your enjoyment."

But she was really too tired to spar with him any more now. He helped her out of the carriage, gave her a fleeting peck on the cheek and waited a moment while she inserted her iron key into the gate – the "hole in the wall."

Then he had leapt back into the carriage and was driving off.

In the Casa Rosa, she stood for a moment or two in the living room, dazed not so much with tiredness and fatigue as with the dream-like happenings of the day.

Martin called out, "That you, Rianna?"

"No. Only us mice!" she called back, and went into his bedroom.

"Gosh! I thought you were lost down in the wine-vaults," he said. "I hope you've got a good story with pictures of your visit."

She giggled. "Oh, I've a good story all right. But we finished that hours ago. Did the chauffeur deliver all the publicity material?"

"Yes, stacks of stuff – and two of your cameras. I wonder you trusted the fellow with those."

"He was the Cavallinis' chauffeur and it was Holford who gave him instructions."

"And I suppose you've been out on the town with Holford all this time."

"Yes, we had dinner together." She made her voice sound casual.

"And supper, too?" he queried with a lift of his eyebrows.

"Heavens! You *are* playing the elder brother. We went to a place inland, a kind of restaurant in a tower."

"Oh, yes, I've heard about that place. People say it's unique and worth visiting."

She rose from the foot of his bed. "Goodnight, Martin. I must confess I'm dead tired. See you in the morning."

In her room she sat at the dressing-table and was slightly shocked at her untidy appearance, her weary-looking face and wind-blown hair. Yet how could she suppress that undoubted sparkle in her sherry-brown eyes? For a few moments she sat motionless, savouring the delights of the high spots of the day. Had she made any real progress with Holford, or was it no more than a single day's enjoyment for him?

She longed to know some of his thoughts as he rode home to the Villa Aurelia in the horse-carriage. Yet she knew this would be beyond her dreams and guesses. It would take a long time to understand this enigmatic man who had so easily captured her heart.

She rose from the dressing-stool and put her hand into the pocket of her jacket. Something small and hard was there. The amber ear-ring! She stared at it. So he had only pretended to throw it into the harbour.

She hastily searched the box where she kept her trinkets and here was the fellow one. She smiled to herself. She ought to have known that he would play a trick on her.

Slowly she put the pair away. She would never wear them again until – but no, that was a foolish dream that had little hopes of ever coming true.

CHAPTER SEVEN

"HAVE you thought any more about this question of hiring a small car while we're here?" Martin asked his sister next morning.

"Yes, I have, and I think it would be a good idea. We could both use it, and after all, I expect to spend more time based on Marsala than anywhere else. We've taken this villa for the six months, so we must make use of it and not stay in hotels elsewhere when it isn't necessary."

Martin nodded. "Right. Then we'll go this morning and see what we can find. Duncan recommended me to a good place."

After inspection of a number of cars at a central garage, Martin finally chose a small Fiat. "Do you think this would suit you, Rianna? Not too difficult to drive, I think."

Where cars were concerned, she knew she could rely on her brother's judgment. "Yes, it's very similar to the one I used at Trapani."

He paid the charge for a month. "We'll go to the Villa Aurelia and try it out," he suggested. "I've some indexing I want you to do for me."

One room at the villa had apparently been set aside for the men to use as a common study where they could work on their own projects undisturbed. Each member of the team had his own table for books and papers and in one corner was a typewriter for anyone to use.

Rianna and Martin settled down to work on arranging a record of the various sequences of camera shots he had taken on different dives.

"Will Holford allow you to show these films other than as

part of one of his own programmes?" she asked.

"That depends. Many of them are part of his initial work, but he says he doesn't mind if I want excerpts sometimes, or even take one or two sequences myself."

"But when could you do that? You're not allowed to dive alone, are you?"

"Certainly not. I've had that lesson knocked into me enough times. But as long as I take a mate with me, I should be in no danger."

Duncan came into the room then. "Hallo, Rianna. Seems a long time since I saw you last."

She smiled. "Three or four days, I think."

"Probably seems longer." He grinned at her. "Mind if I do a spot of work here?" He turned towards Martin. "I have to keep up the log book and also work out the depths for diving when we go around to Syracuse."

"That's all right. You won't disturb us," agreed Martin easily.

Rianna caught the quizzical look that Duncan threw her, but she made no remark.

The three worked until someone called out that lunch was ready.

Rianna glanced at Martin. "Is it all right for me to stay uninvited?"

"Of course! You're one of us, aren't you?"

"You must be my guest," broke in Duncan with a laugh. "Come, Rianna, let me escort you." He held out his arm in an exaggerated gesture, but with a smile she refused to take it.

In some ways she was glad that Holford was absent from the meal, for after last night's unexpected outing to the tower, it would have been slightly difficult for her to face him with a casual manner.

Lynda did not appear until the others were halfway through lunch. "Oh, Rianna! I'd no idea you were here. Why didn't you let me know?"

"Sorry. I came with Martin to do some work and I wasn't sure whether you were at home."

Lynda sat down in her place and frowned. "I'm always at home, it seems. No one bothers to take me anywhere or give me any pleasure."

Duncan said heartily, "Learn to swim and we'll take you down with us on our dives."

She shuddered delicately. "Dry land is better for me." She glared at Duncan. "And it isn't likely that I would ever *want* to dive."

An embarrassed silence followed Duncan's tactless remark. All the same, Rianna considered that Lynda lost no opportunity of reminding everyone of her loss.

Jeffrey started a conversation with Martin about some of his marine specimens and the tension lifted.

After a while Lynda asked Rianna, "How did you enjoy your visit to Emilia's wine-cellars?"

"One of the most interesting places I've been to," replied Rianna quickly.

"And was Emilia there?"

"Part of the time, yes. She gave me brochures and other publicity material."

Lynda began to fiddle with the food on her plate and refrained from asking any more questions. Rianna had expected searching queries as to whether Holford was at the Cavallinis' accompanying her on the tour, but apparently Lynda was temporarily satisfied.

After lunch the men sat for a while on the sun terrace with their coffee and cigarettes. Lynda did not join them and when she had finished her coffee, Rianna returned to the "common room" to continue with Martin's work.

She had been engrossed in her task for perhaps an hour when somewhere close by the window she could hear angry voices. Holford's harsh and decisive, Lynda's high-pitched and tearful.

"Why couldn't I come to the wine place?" Lynda demanded furiously. "And then you —"

Rianna could not escape from the room without betraying her presence, but she put her hands over her ears. Even then the muffled words came incoherently, mainly from Lynda. ". . . you didn't come home to dinner even then ... suppose you took *her* somewhere exciting ... of course, never me ..."

"Lynda, for heaven's sake! Have I to account to you for every movement?"

"You could be nice to me – sometimes." Lynda's voice was wheedling now. "If only for the sake of ..."

There was a low-voiced muttering, then a sharp wail, "Oh, Holford, don't leave me!"

A few moments later Holford came striding into the room where Rianna was working. She glanced up.

"Oh, sorry. I didn't know anyone was here," he said brusquely.

Before she could say anything, he had gone out and slammed the door.

Then a hush descended on the household until Duncan came to the "common room".

"Still working?" he queried fatuously.

"As you see," she replied calmly.

"Then finish soon and come out into the garden." He sat opposite her in Martin's chair.

"All right. Let me get on with it and I'll be through all the sooner."

"Did you hear anything of that unholy row going on outside here?"

"No. What was that?"

Duncan stretched out his legs in front. "Oh, merely Lynda going off the deep end with Holford. She thinks he took someone out to dinner last night, but she can't be sure if it was you or Emilia."

"Or even a girl called Rosa or Bianca or Maria?"

"My guess is that the girl's name was –"

"Sh! Keep your guesses to yourself, Duncan."

He began to laugh quietly, gazing at her out of the corner of his eye. "You've told me what I wanted to know – Lynda would like to know, too, but I won't let it out. Although I'm damned annoyed that I didn't have the chance of taking you. I'll remedy that pretty soon."

"Threat or promise?" she queried.

"Both, perhaps. I don't intend to let Holford have it all his own way. After all, he has Lynda — and Emilia — to play off against each other. What more does the man want?"

"How should I know?" she murmured.

"Then come out to dinner with me tonight. I know several good places, all very respectable."

"I'll have to let you know later, Duncan," she said, trying to temporise. "I'm not sure what Martin's plans are."

"Oh, Martin — he doesn't count." Duncan waved his hand as though to obliterate a mere brother.

"His work does. He and I are a team just as much as all of you are with Holford."

"All right, I'll join the queue. My dinner-date tomorrow, re-member." He rose, then bent down to give her two light taps on the head. As he reached the door, the Italian housekeeper knocked and came in.

"The Signora would like you to have tea with her," the woman told Rianna, who understood enough Italian for that.

"Royal command!" mocked Duncan as he went out.

"Now?" queried Rianna.

"*Si, signorina.*" Rianna followed the housekeeper, but instead of the drawing room, the woman conducted her to Lynda's bed-room.

Lynda was lying on a chaise-longue near the window that led to a balcony.

"Oh, come in, Rianna. I'm so desperately needing company, so you must take pity on me and never mind that bothersome work you're supposed to be doing."

In a few moments the housekeeper brought a tray of tea, with biscuits and little cakes. For a short time the two girls made small talk over their cups of tea, but Rianna was uneasily aware that a storm was not far off.

If she could escape before the storm broke, it would be an advantage. But evidently Lynda guessed what was in Rianna's mind.

Rianna rose to go, but Lynda pleaded, "Stay a little longer with me, Rianna." When Rianna obeyed, Lynda's attitude hardened. "I hear you had a most interesting day yesterday," she began, with a steely look in her light eyes.

"Yes, I enjoyed it very much. I gained a great deal of information."

"And finished up the evening with Holford? That, too, I suppose you enjoyed?"

For a moment Rianna hesitated. She did not want to sound boastful about having secured Holford's company, yet neither did she want to play it down as of little account.

"Well?" prompted Lynda. "Don't tell me you were taken wherever it was by force."

Rianna smiled calmly. "No, of course not. Naturally I enjoyed a visit to such an interesting old place."

Lynda's languid air immediately vanished. She sat upright on the chaise-longue and glared at Rianna. "You must never believe Holford is at all serious about you." Her eyes flashed with malevolence. "He may squire girls here and there, even flirt with them occasionally – but in the end, he comes back to me – as he will always come back."

Rianna remained silent, unwilling to add fuel to Lynda's anger, but that apparently was a mistake, for Lynda immediately interpreted that silence in her own way.

"Of course you're in love with him! I've known that since I first came here. You can't deny it!"

"And are you in love with him?" asked Rianna quietly, but with some steeliness in her tone.

Lynda's eyes opened to their fullest extent. "How could you ask such an inane question? Of course – I've loved him for years and years, long before I knew Jack. And Holford loved me." She rose jerkily and began to walk about the room. "I was a fool, oh, yes, a fool several times over. I was upset with Holford over some small thing – I forget what it was now – and I encouraged Jack just to make Holford jealous. Before I knew what was happening, I'd agreed to marry Jack. He was so desperately in love with me that I suppose I really took pity on him."

When she paused as if in recollection, Rianna asked softly, "And Holford? What was his reaction?"

"Oh, he cast me off utterly. Told me that if I wanted to marry Jack to go ahead. But I was never happy with Jack. All the time my heart longed for Holford. I saw him only two or three times after I'd married Jack and then Holford was difficult to understand. Sometimes I thought he was cold as ice and at others I was sure he still loved me as much as ever. Then the men went off to the Pacific and Jack was cameraman. I never saw him again."

Even though most of Lynda's ideas were entirely repugnant to her, Rianna could not help the feeling of compassion that blotted out her antipathy. "That was very sad for you," she murmured.

Lynda turned sharply to face Rianna. "Oh, you needn't feel so sorry for me. In a way, it was a blessing in disguise. Sooner or later, I'd have divorced Jack – and then been free to marry Holford."

Rianna frowned. "But Jack surely didn't have to die to set you free from an unhappy marriage? Divorce would have answered, surely."

Lynda smiled. "You don't understand. Holford was desperate, too, to find a way out of the tangle – and he took it. It was the only solution."

Rianna jumped to her feet. "Lynda, what are you saying? Are you accusing Holford of – of contriving an accident that would drown Jack and free you?"

Lynda pursed her lips. "Well, he may not have actually thought it out like that, but the result was the same. Only Holford and no one else was responsible for the accident – if it was an accident –"

"Wasn't there an inquest or some sort of inquiry?"

"Oh, yes, but in some foreign country where these matters are dealt with in a haphazard manner. I was too ill at the time to fly out to Borneo or wherever it was, but later Holford flew home to tell me about what had happened."

"Did Holford really take the blame – or did you put that blame fairly and squarely on his shoulders?" Rianna demanded.

"There was no need. He attended to all the details for me –

like insurance and so on – so that I shouldn't be left destitute. Also, he's undertaken to pay for the education of my son, Terry."

Rianna noted that this was the first time Lynda had ever mentioned the boy.

Lynda was reclining again on the chaise-longue. "Some people would say that he was undertaking more obligation than he need – and that Terry might be his own son – but –"

"Lynda!" Rianna interrupted sharply. "How can you expect me to believe you have a single shred of love for Holford if you make these vile accusations against him?"

"It hurts you, doesn't it, to find your idol might not be quite so perfect as you imagine. But you'll find in the end that he'll turn to me and there's nothing you can do about it. Nor can that Italian girl, Emilia. Oh, I know he was starting up a very promising friendship with her, but as soon as I appeared here, he forgot all about her. Actually, it makes it easier if I have two possible rivals, you and Emilia."

"Easier for whom?" inquired Rianna coldly.

"For me!" A triumphant gleam appeared in Lynda's hard eyes. "It amuses Holford very much to see you and this Italian girl at loggerheads with each other and competing for his favours."

"Emilia and I are certainly not at loggerheads with each other," Rianna contradicted smartly, "and I very much doubt if Emilia is indeed one of your rivals. It's much more likely that she'll marry one of her own nationality."

Lynda looked up slyly. "Then that leaves only you, Rianna."

Rianna flushed slightly, aware that she had focussed Lynda's attention on herself. "I think you need have no fears that I should ever be able to take Holford from you," she said quietly. "If, that is, he can be regarded as your property."

Lynda was on her feet, her face contorted with fury. "I have every claim to him!" she shouted. "He's mine and nobody else's."

Rianna surveyed the other girl as calmly as she could. "Holford is not a prize packet to be wrestled for. He's an independent man with some independence of action." Then she was astoun-

128

ded to hear herself saying, "If you want to succeed with him, Lynda, then you might try to stop clinging to him so much." Why on earth should she give advice to this girl who had no real love for Holford but was intent only on wresting some security from him?

But Lynda was equal to the taunt. "Why? Have you tried the clinging technique yourself?"

"I'm hardly the clinging type," retorted Rianna.

Lynda smiled. "No, you're not. Now let me give you some advice. Men don't take kindly to girls who are too competent and practical and think they know it all. You've no finesse, I suppose that's why you haven't yet found a man to marry you."

"How do you know that I've looked?" Rianna countered. She walked towards the door and turned. "If you don't mind, I'll get back to my work downstairs. Thank you for the tea."

She found it difficult to settle again to the work of indexing and making notes for Martin. The scene with Lynda had perturbed her more than she wanted to admit. ". . . too competent and practical . . . think they know it all . . ." The other girl's words echoed in Rianna's mind with uncomfortable precision. Was it true that perhaps Holford regarded her only as a competent, feminine adjunct to his team? Someone doing the kind of work that was not worth the while of an expert diver? She remembered that when she had accompanied him to the tower inn he had taken it for granted that she was level-headed enough to withstand heights. She wondered now if there had been an underlying implication in his words.

She was glad when it was time for Martin to go to the gymnasium for his daily swimming and other exercises.

"Shall I drive you there?" he asked. "Then you can take the car home, but don't knock it about. I shall need it tonight."

"When did I ever knock cars about?" she demanded, laughing.

"Remember that gate you cannoned into when we went to –"

"Yes, all right. That was a long time ago when I was a novice."

When she reached the Casa Rosa, it occurred to her that she had not asked her brother why he needed the car tonight, but when he came in later the reason was obvious. No, he didn't need

129

dinner, and had she seen that dark red tie that he'd bought a week ago?

Spruced up in fawn trousers and a new blazer, his hair tidy and a sparkle in his grey eyes – it was quite apparent to a sisterly eye that he was off to meet his date.

"Someone you've met here?" she asked casually, as she busied herself with her own meal.

"Where else? Or do you think she's a stowaway we keep on the yacht?" He picked up a breadstick and munched it. "Don't wait up. I might be late."

"Take care of yourself, then," she warned. "And, of course, the lady."

He grinned cheekily at her as he went out to the courtyard and through to the street.

After Rianna had finished her dinner and cleared away, she was assailed by a restless feeling – or was it loneliness because she was shut out of the companionship of the circle at the Villa Aurelia? Surely she could not expect Holford or someone else to take her out to dinner every night? Her thoughts veered to Lynda who was in residence at Holford's villa and no doubt enjoyed the company of one or other of the men every night.

Rianna pushed aside these envious thoughts. If she didn't take care, she'd find herself aping Lynda and clamouring for masculine company at any price.

She made a pot of coffee and took it out to the courtyard. Martin had rigged up a table lamp on a long flex so that it could be plugged in inside the house. She was reading a Sicilian newspaper when someone knocked on the courtyard door.

Her first thoughts were for Martin. An accident? Or perhaps he had returned for something? But it was Holford who stood there, his face composed and unsmiling.

"May I come in?"

She realised that she had been holding the rough wooden door and almost blocking his entrance. "Yes, of course. Yes, come in."

She wondered what was the object of his visit but assumed that he had not come to acquaint her with bad news.

"Coffee?" she offered, as he sat at the garden table on one of the chairs he had himself given her.

He nodded and took the cup almost absentmindedly.

"Is Martin in?" he asked after a few minutes.

"No, he's out somewhere." Rianna was too discreet to disclose that her brother was no doubt accompanied by a girl.

"What sort of day did you have at the Aurelia?" It was a curious question, she thought.

"All right," she answered guardedly. "I did a fair amount of work for Martin on the various shots. I haven't begun on any connected commentary yet."

There was a long pause. Then he said, "Whenever we have the yacht in harbour and it's handy for you, I think you might work on board sometimes, but that's up to you. It might save Martin having to bring so much detail ashore."

"Thank you. Yes, it might be a help – to him." She was at a loss to understand his reasons, but in a moment or two his meaning was clarified.

"I gather there was a bit of a scene with Lynda today and I don't want any unpleasantness to happen again."

Her anger rose instantly. So she was now to be banished from any contact with the Villa Aurelia and its occupants and do her work in isolation on the yacht!

"I can just as easily work at home here," she said coolly. "Martin can bring me the notes and details."

He turned to look at her, his features sharpened in the lamplight. "A moment ago you agreed that working on the yacht might be an advantage. Why change your mind?"

"I'm sorry if Lynda was upset today, but she asked me up to her room for tea. If you don't want me to go to the Aurelia because of Lynda, then please say so honestly."

Surprisingly, he stretched out his hand and closed it over her wrist, and his warm touch fired her blood. Her anger vanished, but she called herself several sorts of coward.

"Rianna, why do you misunderstand everything I say? It's because I want to save you from Lynda's tantrums that I suggested –"

"Oh, I thought you were blaming me for grieving her. I know she's frail and has suffered a great deal."

He withdrew his hand and thrust his elbows on the table, resting his chin on his clasped hands. "I came here for an hour's peace and quiet. Don't tell me I've come to the wrong address."

She kept her head down so that he should not see the sudden gladness on her face. "I'll get you some brandy," she suggested, seeking an excuse to go away from him for a few moments so that she might recover her composure.

She returned with the brandy and poured the glasses. "Only the inexpensive kind, I'm afraid."

Then a new thought came into her head. "Perhaps I shouldn't have offered you alcohol. Does it affect your diving if you practise next day?"

He held up the small glass towards the light. "Not in really moderate quantities, but we try not to drink for some hours before diving."

"Like car driving," she said lightly. "Don't drink *and* drive."

For the next few minutes he remained silent and she did not disturb him. She was overjoyed that apparently he had sought her company when he needed to relax.

Then he leaned towards her across the table and the lamp shone harshly on his face, highlighting the ridge of his nose and the serious downward curve of his mouth.

"Rianna, are you content to trust your brother to me? You're certainly aware that one of my previous cameramen was drowned in an unfortunate accident."

"Yes, I've been told."

"By whom?" he queried.

She hesitated. "Does that matter?"

"Yes, it does matter. You may have heard quite different versions according to the teller. Duncan, no doubt, told you what he knew. And Lynda?"

"Yes. No one else."

"The truth is – and I've always faced it – that I was entirely responsible for Jack's death. I don't want to go into details, but the plain fact is that I should have taken more care."

132

"But it was an accident. You couldn't have been entirely to blame."

"An accident, yes, but accidents are often caused by carelessness or a lack of foresight or sometimes unexpected situations." He sighed deeply.

"Perhaps in time you won't feel so responsible," she said quietly, trying to reassure him.

"It's Lynda's loss that worries me. I deprived her of Jack and I can never forgive myself for this. Nor can I ever forget the responsibility I owe to her."

Rianna reflected that Lynda was determined to make sure that Holford would never forget for a single moment what he owed to her.

"But even Lynda might find happiness at some time in the future," Rianna pointed out.

"Lynda feels that her future happiness lies with me," he said flatly, looking away across the courtyard. "She wants me to marry her."

"But if you marry her out of duty, where will any future happiness lie?" queried Rianna in a leaden voice.

He turned towards her and half smiled. "Nowhere. Of course I'd do my best to make Lynda happy, but –"

"Is it true that you and Lynda were engaged years ago?"

"Who told you that? We were never engaged. I knew her, certainly, but only because she was Jack's fiancée."

"I see." Rianna was digesting this awkward-shaped piece of the jigsaw. Lynda had so emphatically declared that she and Holford had been engaged.

After a moment or two he said, "I don't know why I've come here to bore you with my personal problems, but –"

"I'm not in the least bored," she interrupted quickly. "I wish I could help you. I hope that you can always count on me as a friend to whom you can talk in confidence."

While she said the words, her whole being was in revolt. She did not in the least desire to be his woman confidante, the soft shoulder on which he could lay his head when in trouble. Well, yes, perhaps she did want to be able to comfort him, but she longed for a good deal more than that. She would never be content with a minor rôle on the fringe of his life. Better to cut adrift altogether, go back to England and forget about him.

"Thank you, Rianna," he murmured. "I'll remember that."

In her mind she was groping about for the right words to clothe a daring suggestion. At last she said, "Supposing you became involved with – with another girl, someone you loved and wanted to marry, how would that affect Lynda?"

His mouth took on a grim line. "That possibility is something I have to shut away very completely." He gave her a quick friendly smile. "Oh, I'm not pretending that the idea might not have occurred to me before now. I'm twenty-eight and I've known one or two girls. Sometimes I've felt inclined to take the plunge and settle down, but the kind of work I do is not only exacting, but demands a wife who is very tolerant, self-sacrificing even."

She was tempted to rap out that he was not likely to achieve that kind of wife with Lynda, yet his next words ripped across that idea of hers.

"Lynda does know what's involved in my kind of career. With all her faults and imperfections, she understands the set-up."

Rianna could only assume that there were hidden virtues in Lynda's character that she herself had not been able to experience. Aloud she said, "Would Lynda be able to travel around with you and the team? I thought she wasn't strong enough for that."

"That's true. She's not exactly robust. Then again, she has a son in England. Jack's mother is looking after the boy at present, but Lynda would naturally feel that she ought to be with her child."

"Nothing of the sort!" The words were out before Rianna could stop them and Holford stared across the table at her.

"I'm sorry. I shouldn't have said that," she apologised.

"But you meant what you said. You don't like Lynda, do you?"

She glanced away, her face flaming with embarrassment, but out of the lamplight he would not be able to see her confusion. "It's not a question of liking or disliking her," she said slowly.

"I don't see eye to eye with her on some subjects, but it's not for me to pass judgment on her. I expect I can tolerate her most of the time."

"I'm surprised. I thought you two might have a lot in common and when the team were away on the yacht or elsewhere, you and Lynda would have some pleasant times together."

How blind could a man be! Did he never suspect that Lynda was not particularly interested in women, unless they threatened her future plans? She liked men to admire and flatter her, dance attendance on her and act at all times with gallantry.

Rianna smiled at him, although her facial muscles had to be coaxed into such a shape "It seems I must remind you that I really did come here with Martin to help him in his work. Also, I have my own to occupy me, so I've only a limited time for leisure and pleasure."

He nodded, yet there was a certain coolness about his expression. "Of course. I really must get it into my head that you're not the pleasure-seeking holiday girl, but strictly practical-minded." He rose to go. "Well, thanks for listening to me, Rianna. I hope I haven't prevented you from doing something else more important."

She could not exactly quarrel with his words, but his tone certainly implied a hint of sarcasm.

She accompanied him to the door in the courtyard wall. "Goodnight, Holford. I'm glad you came."

He held her hand for an instant. *"Buona notte."* He lingered against the door opening, reluctant to leave, it seemed. "I must sort out my own problems, of course. Actually, there was a girl – a third party who might have solved some of my difficulties – but she's otherwise engaged."

In the darkness of the street, Rianna could not see his face. He saluted, called *"Arrivederci"* and was gone.

Rianna shut the door slowly and then leaned against it. She was dazed by so many conflicting emotions. Flattered because he had sought her company and had been glad to unburden himself, but uneasy at the last-minute mention of a girl who might have helped him. When he said "otherwise engaged", did he

135

mean occupied in some other way or literally that she was attached to another man? A girl back in England or one here in Sicily? He could mean only Emilia. All the hints of Holford's attraction to the lovely Italian girl now rushed together in Rianna's mind into one definite fact. He seemed to be on excellent terms with Emilia's father, but that did not necessarily imply that he would be regarded as an eligible husband for Emilia. It might also be that Emilia had definite ideas of the man she wanted to marry.

Rianna walked across the courtyard, cleared away the coffee cups and eventually prepared herself for bed.

Martin could let himself in whenever he chose to return.

Rianna began to laugh quietly to herself. What an extraordinary position! The man to whom she had given her love, even though against her will, had come tonight to disclose his dilemma, his unwillingness to marry Lynda and his hopeless attraction for another girl, almost undoubtedly Emilia.

All it needed now was for Martin to fall hopelessly in love with some girl here and cause further complications.

She was still awake when he came home.

"Had a good evening?" she called.

"The best in the world. See you in the morning."

Obviously he was not prepared to confide in her tonight, and perhaps that was just as well. She had received enough confidences for one night.

CHAPTER EIGHT

WHEN Martin came home to dinner the next evening he seemed to be in a disgruntled mood.

"Anything wrong?" asked Rianna mildly, aware as always of her brother's temperament.

"I've instructions for you. Holford says that if you ever want to start skin-diving, or even later on, scuba, you must practise more swimming. Every day."

"Where? In the sea?"

"Preferably at the gymnasium."

"I didn't know they allowed women there."

"There are two pools there, one for men and one mixed," he told her.

Rianna helped herself to cheese and biscuits. "H'm. I'm not sure that I want to be that venturesome."

"Well, if you want to write about the underwater marvels of the ocean, you've got to look at a small piece of it first-hand."

"I'll think about it," she promised.

"That's one piece of news. The second is that Emilia has invited the lot of us up to her family villa for dancing tomorrow night."

"Including me?"

"Oh, certainly including you. How could you be left out and disappoint Duncan?"

"Is it to be a very dressy occasion?" she asked, aware of her still fairly limited wardrobe.

"I shouldn't think so. One of your long slinky skirts might be adequate."

"With a suitable top, of course," she amended.

"This affair is apparently meant to be a grand send-off before the boys go to Syracuse."

"Do you know where the house is?"

"Not exactly, but the others will tell me, and anyway, Lynda has stayed there. By the way, did Holford come here last night?"

"Yes. About nine or half-past?"

"Did you tell him where I'd gone?"

"How could I? I didn't know. I didn't say you were taking a girl out for the evening. Only that you were out."

Martin remained thoughtful for a few moments, then drank some wine.

"Why? Did he want to see you for any reason?" she asked.

He frowned. "No. But he went off the deep end at me because – well – er – my companion was Emilia."

"Emilia?" echoed Rianna, immediately apprehensive of repercussions where Holford was concerned in connection with the Italian girl.

"There was an unholy row when he found out," continued Martin. "Not so much over who my companion was, but where I'd taken her."

"And where was that?"

Martin chuckled. "You know how hedged around she is with all the taboos and restrictions because she's a Sicilian girl. She told me that most Italian girls now have some freedom, but Sicilian fathers keep a stricter eye on their daughters. She hinted that she longed to see the cabaret show at a restaurant called the Angelo. So I took her there last night in all innocence."

"And was it a crime?"

"According to Holford, yes. He commanded me to say nothing to anyone about such an escapade. No doubt Emilia had made a very innocuous excuse for her absence and the time she arrived home. Actually, she made me drop her quite a few yards from the entrance to her house in Marsala, but I watched her go in at the gate, so she was safe enough."

Rianna was silent for a few moments. Then she said, "And you're not to take Emilia again to such dens of vice. Is that it? Or aren't you to be allowed to take her out at all?"

Martin grimaced. "It dawned on me afterwards that the big chief himself has his eye on her and doesn't want undercutting competition from the likes of me."

"I wonder. I really think that Emilia will eventually be reserved for some handsome Italian or Sicilian of noble family and none of the English hopefuls will get a look in."

She hoped her light remark would disarm any suspicions that Martin might have about Holford's attraction to Emilia, although by now she knew this to be the unpalatable truth.

"Anyway, I was also caned for visiting the place myself, although it was respectable enough, it seemed to me. But he's afraid I might drink too much at nights and upset his diving schedule. So I'm to stay home and be a good little boy and drink lemonade."

Rianna laughed. "I'm sure he's not as tyrannical as that. Moderation is all he really insists on."

"Well, he should trust me not to overstep the mark. I've my own safety to think of. Actually, Steve, our M.O. chap, was telling me the other day about Jack Patterson, Lynda's husband."

"What did he tell you?" queried Rianna calmly. She had been most careful up to now to shield her brother from too much casual information about that previous tragedy, especially information that might not even be true.

"That he had warned Jack several times about drinking rather too much, especially shortly before diving."

"I see," commented Rianna, afraid to add anything further, but her mind was busily roaming over the way Holford had shouldered the entire blame. Now of course he was doubly cautious about the members of his team.

When Martin was ready to leave for the gymnasium, she said quickly, "Wait for me! I'll come down in the car to the shops and see if I can buy a new dress."

"You're always buying clothes!" he grumbled. "How will the money last out if you keep squandering it?"

She laughed. "Whose money is it, I'd like to know? As for you, wining and dining girls of Emilia's standard –"

"All right, you win."

The next evening she took considerable time over dressing and make-up. She was pleased with the new dress, a long pleated skirt in a stained-glass-window pattern where the predominant colours were peacock, emerald and gold, worn with a matching blouse with long sleeves gathered at the wrist.

The amber ear-rings would go well, she considered, but she had made a vow never to wear them again unless – or until – but now, it seemed, she would have no further use for them. Instead, she wore some small Toledo studs of black and gold, brushed her hair into loose waves that would catch the light, perhaps, and glow with reddish tints. Gold sandals and a lightweight stole completed her outfit, but she thought it prudent to sit in the back of the car instead of alongside Martin.

"I should hate to get my skirt wound around your hand-brake," she told him.

"You're obviously out to conquer," he teased. "Which is it to be? Duncan or Jeffrey? Or even Holford?"

"Drive on, James," she instructed him tersely, "and don't chatter. I hope you know the way. My shoes are not designed for hill climbing."

The Cavallini villa was about six or seven miles out of Marsala, just off the coast road and on a slight rise overlooking the sea.

Rianna remembered Lynda's enthusiasm about its luxurious atmosphere and regretted that the garden was too dim to see the colours of flowers and trees. The house was large and built of pale coloured stone, Rianna supposed, and a blaze of light streamed from the tall ground floor windows.

Emilia came forward to greet Rianna and her brother.

"You are both most welcome," she said. "There will be friends of yours here, but you must also meet some of mine."

She introduced Rianna to a succession of engagingly handsome young men, a couple of girls, several older people.

"My father you have met many times." Then Emilia drifted away to attend to other guests.

Signor Cavallini wanted to know how the photographs had come out. "Those you took at the wine-vaults. You have made me look fat?" he queried with throaty chuckles.

"Not in the least," she replied, remembering how she had grouped the people that day. "I will bring a print and prove to you how slim you look." She took a glass of light dry wine from the proffered tray.

"One of our own blend," Signor Cavallini told her. "From our own vines that grow behind this house."

She sipped the pale golden liquid. "Then it can really be called 'local' when it is from your own vineyards."

"Now you must talk to the young men," he said with a gallant bow. "There are many who would wish to speak with you."

For a moment she was left alone, a single figure among small groups. Then Duncan was by her side.

"You look stunning!" he complimented her. "What a colour sense you have!"

"Flatterer! What do you hope to gain?"

"A good question, but not one that I intend to answer – yet. When the dancing begins, I shall expect your co-operation."

"I'm against monopolies," she retorted with a smile.

"We'll see." He looked across the room. "Lynda is in her element at the moment."

Rianna glanced in the direction he indicated. Lynda was almost surrounded by seven or eight young men and appeared to be in one of her gayest moods. She was wearing a bright flame dress that overpowered her pale, fragile looks.

Maids and menservants handed delicious morsels of food and at one side of the room was a long buffet for those who preferred to help themselves.

After about half an hour evidently the signal had been given that the dancing could begin and the guests drifted away in twos and threes towards a ballroom large enough to grace the average town hall. An orchestra was already playing softly to encourage dancers on to the floor, but apparently everyone was waiting for Emilia to open. When she came through the elaborately-carved double doors, she twirled herself around three times, as in blind man's buff, then stretched her hand to the nearest man. The man happened to be Holford.

141

Rianna momentarily closed her eyes as the searing pain tore at her heart. Was any further proof needed that whatever difficulties might lie in the way? Holford and Emilia were mutually attracted to each other. Emilia herself had revealed earlier that some of her family had married English partners. In fact, much of the wine industry in Marsala had been founded by English firms in the first place. Whatever objections the Cavallinis might raise, Holford could not be rejected merely because he was English.

Without her knowing it, Duncan had swept her into his arms and she was moving her feet rhythmically in a waltz.

"Aren't you rather far away?" she heard him whisper. "A man likes to feel that he's dancing with a real live girl, and not a shadowy wraith that will vanish and leave him holding nothing."

"I'm sorry, Duncan. I was thinking of something else."

"Or someone else?" He tightened his arm around her. "Forget him. Concentrate on me for a change."

"What makes you think you're worth the effort?" she queried, smiling.

"Every man has his own value."

"But that's only his opinion, his self-inflation."

It was good, she reflected, to be able to talk lightly to Duncan without having to weigh her words in case the listener might put a different meaning on them.

During the evening she danced with numerous partners, Jeffrey, Steve and several of the young Italians, but not once with Holford. Once she saw him with Lynda, but several times when she glanced around the room she could not see him.

Then later when she was sitting out with Duncan on the wide, balustraded terrace, lit with small lanterns in the shape of torches, there came floating out the sound of someone singing.

"Emilia!" said Rianna. "Let's go in and listen."

Duncan was reluctant, evidently preferring Rianna's company to Emilia's glorious voice, but Rianna moved swiftly through the open french windows and stood among a group of people in a corner. Emilia was standing close to the grand piano, but with yet another pang Rianna now saw that Holford was accompanying. Tonight the lesson was certainly being hammered home that Holford and Emilia were in sympathetic accord, for the smile that the singer bestowed on her accompanist at the end of the song held more than mere thanks for his aid.

In response to the applause, Emilia obliged with two more songs, an aria from the opera *Norma* by Bellini, the Sicilian composer, followed by an amusing Sicilian song which delighted her audience, although the humour was lost on Rianna.

When the dancing began again, Holford came towards her. "I've kept seeing you from afar," he murmured, "but when I looked again, you'd disappeared. Enjoying the evening?"

"Yes, very much," she answered conventionally. So he had looked for her? Not very eagerly, she decided. He had been too busy with Emilia, Lynda and possibly other girls to give Rianna much passing attention. Even now he was probably awarding her a duty dance for the sake of appearances. Then she tried to snap out of this self-pitying mood. She was in his arms, as close to him as the propriety of a ballroom could allow. What more did she want? Why not enjoy even a few moments of happiness with him? Unconsciously she relaxed, and as she did so, he must have sensed the change in her attitude, for he grasped her more firmly.

"That's better," he whispered close to her ear. "You were dreaming. I notice you're wearing different ear-rings."

"Would you prefer that I wore odd ones – or only one amber?" She was not prepared to admit that she had discovered the amber ear-ring he had pretended to throw into the harbour.

She was glad of the chance to talk of some trivial matter, for surely he must hear her heart beating wildly, be aware that her body was trembling held so closely against his own.

In one sense she wanted the dance to go on for ever; in another, she was relieved when the music stopped and the dancers drifted from the floor. Holford was leading her outside to the terrace when Lynda came swiftly up to them.

"Oh, Holford! Could you spare a minute? Someone wants to talk to you."

A blatant ruse, thought Rianna, as she watched Lynda cling

prettily to Holford's arm as they walked away. The "someone who wants to talk to you" was no doubt Lynda herself.

But it was towards the end of the evening when Rianna received the most grievous blow. In an interval between dances she had been sitting on the terrace at a table with Duncan and Jeffrey. When the music started again, Duncan rose. "Come on, Rianna. One more waltz. It's probably the last of the evening. It's nearly midnight and Holford will probably send us all home like Cinderella on the stroke of twelve."

She agreed, and as she accompanied him towards the ballroom she paused to gaze at the moon's shining pathway reflected on the sea.

"Romantic, isn't it?" whispered Duncan, putting his arm around her. "Those two up there evidently think so, too."

Farther along the terrace two people stood against a column. The moon's radiance shone clearly on Emilia's lovely features, on her golden dress, silvering it to a metallic sheen. The man's back was toward Rianna, but as though in response to a secret signal, he half turned towards Emilia and removed the last vestige of uncertainty in Rianna's mind. Holford, of course.

"I think I'm too tired to dance again," she apologised to Duncan.

"Then we'll find somewhere to sit out here. After all, the night was made for music – and dancing – and romance."

"If you don't mind, I'll go indoors and find Martin."

"Determined to give me the slip? I can drive you home just as well as Martin can."

She smiled at him. "Perhaps that's what I'm afraid of."

"My driving ability? I assure you I drive very well." He pulled her gently towards him. "Why won't you give me a chance, Rianna?"

"A chance of what?"

"Showing you that there's more than one pebble on the beach. You've got this obsession about Holford and where will it lead you? You don't really have to worry too much about Emilia. Lynda's the one who will pip you in the end."

She knew that he spoke common sense, yet his way of expres-

144

sing what might eventually be true grated on her nerves.

"How do you know I have this obsession, as you call it?"

He laughed softly. "It shows, my dear. It shows in every expression of your face, every inflection of your voice. I'd be delighted if you displayed as much for me."

She recovered some of her poise. What was the use of exposing her hidden desires to someone like Duncan?

"You wouldn't be in the least impressed," she said with more animation. "You've already determined to remain a bachelor for the next few years."

"Not true. Perhaps it was until you came along."

"Nonsense! You have the perfect excuse – your diving. It wouldn't be fair to a wife while you have to go all over the globe plunging into the depths of the sea."

He chuckled. "You don't mince words. Perhaps that's one of the things I like about you."

Further argument was saved by the appearance of Martin. "Oh, there you are, Rianna! I was looking in all sorts of odd corners where I thought you might be tucked away with one or other of your innumerable partners. Ready to go?"

"Yes, quite ready."

"I wasn't successful in inducing her to be tucked away with me in any odd corner," Duncan said with mock dejection.

On the way home, Martin said, "Emilia suggested that you might like to stay a few days at the villa while we're on the trip to Syracuse. You could then join us there, coming overland."

"I can't stay there idling," she protested. "I must get on with some work. I'm not like you and the diving team, pottering about down below and then stretching yourselves out and sunbathe on the yacht."

Martin guffawed. "Fine chance we have of sunbathing! Jeffrey dries out his marine specimens all over the deck. Besides, Holford sees to it that I don't waste time in developing the films, just in case we have to make more dives to get the shots he wants."

When Emilia telephoned next day and Rianna took the call in the adjoining *pensione,* the latter explained her position.

"Then I have another idea," continued Emilia. "I would like to accompany you. I can probably show you some of the interesting sights and tell you about them. I can be your guide."

Rianna hesitated, unwilling to offend Emilia. "Could I have today to think it over?" she eventually compromised. "I'll telephone you tomorrow morning. Will you be at the villa or at your town house in Marsala?"

"Up here," replied Emilia.

When Rianna talked the matter over with Martin, he at once advised her to accept Emilia's offer. "She knows the island and she can save you no end of time."

"I'm puzzled by the fact that she can gaily offer to take me on a three or four-day trip to various towns, when apparently as a Sicilian girl strictly brought up, she has to make excuses to have dinner on board the yacht. Then there was this escapade of yours, taking her to the night-club."

"It wasn't a night-club. Only a cabaret show."

"Still, the fact remains that she had to sneak out of her house – and, as you said, sneak back again when you took her home. I wonder if she's really restricted – or only pretending to be."

"Oh, you can't say that about Emilia. She's as honest as they come. Now if it were Lynda, you might suspect some underhand trickery going on."

"So Emilia is more of a favourite with you than Lynda?" Rianna glanced slyly at her brother.

"Oh, Lynda!" he said disgustedly. "She's no one's favourite. Did you notice last night how she kept dancing with that Italian chap Enrico, friend of Emilia?"

"Did she? Trying to make someone jealous, was she?"

Martin laughed. "Could be. Perhaps Emilia. He's one of her special boy-friends, I think."

Rianna remained silent. Or could it have been Holford? she wondered. Yet last night Holford and Emilia seemed well content with each other's company.

On the day that the yacht *Celestina* left Marsala, Rianna went to the harbour to see the team off. The ship glided away from her moorings and Holford, Martin and Jeffrey were in the bows waving to her. The team would take about six or seven days to sail leisurely round the south coast of the island and up the east to Syracuse.

"We need time to dive every day," Martin had pointed out.

When Rianna turned away from the harbour to return to her own little villa, she was astounded to find Duncan walking towards her.

"But the *Celestina* has gone!" she exclaimed. "You've missed her."

He shook his head and smiled. "No. I'm joining the others at Syracuse. I thought we might go together, since you're planning to visit some of the towns on the way."

"I couldn't do that. I've arranged with Emilia. She's going to act as my guide."

"Emilia? Do you really think her parents will allow her to go off wandering with another girl, staying in strange hotels at nights and facing who knows what mortal dangers?"

"Well, I had given that aspect some thought," she confessed. "But why haven't you gone with the team?"

"I wasn't fit enough. Not for Holford's standards. I started a cold, so I opted out of this trip."

"Well, I'm sorry, Duncan, but I've made arrangements with Emilia. I'm driving up to her villa this afternoon."

"Right. I'll meet you there." He walked off briskly.

While she collected her equipment and clothes for the next few days, Rianna smiled to herself. Duncan must think she was very naïve. She guessed that he must have given some more credible excuse to Holford than a mere cold, even though she knew divers must not risk the slightest illness or injury.

At the Cavallini villa Emilia expressed her delight that Rianna had agreed to the plan.

"My mother will accompany us and, of course, one of our chauffeurs, so there will be no driving for either of us. You can safely leave your car here and someone will drive it to wherever you want it. To Syracuse if you would like that."

Rianna was not accustomed to such de luxe travelling, but of course she saw now that Emilia would necessarily have to be suitably chaperoned.

"It is too late to make a start today," continued Emilia, "so you will stay the night here? We'll start first thing in the morning."

To her discomfort, but not exactly surprise, Rianna found that Lynda was staying at the villa indefinitely while the diving team were away.

"I couldn't stay in that ghastly villa alone with that housekeeper woman," Lynda explained.

Ghastly villa! Rianna thought indignantly. The Villa Aurelia that Holford had rented was probably far more comfortable than anywhere else would be here in Sicily, but naturally, to be staying in even greater luxury at Emilia's home was more attractive to Lynda's self-indulgent nature.

Rianna pulled herself up sharply. She must try not to think so uncharitably of Lynda. She made some vague reply and then strolled around the gardens, as Emilia had invited her to do.

There were numerous short flights of steps, twisting paths and unexpected nooks provided with a stone bench. Trees and tall bushes provided shade, sweet chestnut, birches, black pines, and in contrast to the dark masses of shadow the brilliant colours of flowers dazzled the eye. Rianna could recognise bougainvillea and hibiscus, clambering morning glory and banks of rock rose, but there were many others unfamiliar to her.

She decided to return to the house for one of her cameras. Emilia was sunning herself on the wide terrace.

"You won't mind if I take some photographs of your lovely garden?" asked Rianna.

"We shall be enchanted. Go where you please. I will not accompany you. Then you are free to photograph whatever you choose."

Rianne smiled her thanks. Emilia was one of the most considerate women one could ever meet. If she ever became Holford's wife, he would indeed be lucky.

For the next half hour Rianna wandered around the various paths, up and down the steps, pausing on the occasional small terraces that gave yet another delightful view of the sapphire sea. Then she turned a corner and was confronted by Lynda and Enrico. The young Italian immediately rose and bowed to Rianna, but Lynda's mouth fell open and her face flushed pink.

"You have been photographing the garden?" asked the young man, making the obvious remark.

"And spying on everyone?" muttered Lynda.

"I wasn't expecting to meet people. Even the gardeners are taking their siesta," returned Rianna, ignoring Lynda's thrust.

"Then we shall pose for you," decided Enrico.

"Oh, no!" exclaimed Lynda, apparently with apprehension. "I always photograph so badly."

Enrico turned to look at her. "That is nonsense. You are very pretty."

Rianna hesitated. Her impulse was to extricate herself from this rather curious situation. What was Lynda up to?

Enrico settled the argument. "Come, Lynda, you will sit on the bench, so. I will stand behind –"

Rianna began to laugh. He stood erect and stiff, like someone in a Victorian grouping of husband and wife.

Lynda half turned her face away so that she was in profile. Obviously she was annoyed at being discovered in the company of the handsome young Italian friend of Emilia.

A spark of mischief entered into Rianna. "Smile, please!" she commanded the pair. Enrico smirked and Lynda set her mouth in a mulish expression.

"Thank you!" said Rianna.

Lynda immediately sprang up. "Now let me take you, Rianna. Sit next to Enrico on the bench."

"I'm afraid that was the last of the film," Rianna apologised, slightly ashamed of the lie. But she was not willing to entrust her camera to Lynda, nor did she want to be photographed alongside Enrico. Perhaps it was a sixth sense that warned her that at some future time Lynda might try to make use of an innocuous photograph.

Early in the evening Duncan arrived, surprising everyone except Lynda. Rianna was angry that he had followed her up to Emilia's villa.

"I told you clearly, Duncan, that I had made arrangements with Emilia. I can't break them now – even if I wanted to."

"And obviously you don't want to," he muttered.

"If you must know the truth – that's the answer. I've allowed Emilia to book hotels at several towns. How could I now tell her that I want to travel with you instead?"

Rianna and Duncan were at the corner of one of the terraces where the columns were festooned with climbing roses.

"You do know how to give me the brush-off, don't you?" he growled.

"Look, Duncan," she said patiently, "I do value you as a friend, but you're trying to put me in a totally false position. I can't career about the countryside from town to town and stay with you in hotels as though you were my brother."

"All right, I'll clear off," he said sullenly. "If it were Holford who offered you his company, you wouldn't stop to worry about whether it was proper or not to be staying in the same hotel."

Rianna felt the swift colour mount to her face. She bit back the sharp retort on the edge of her tongue. Duncan's barb was only too true.

"I was asked to stay to dinner, but you can give Emilia my apologies. See you in Syracuse – perhaps."

Rianna remained on the terrace for some minutes, then wished afterwards that she had immediately gone indoors, for Lynda came sidling up, a sweet smile on her face.

"How cruel you were to poor Duncan! You gave him such a slap in the face."

"Did he tell you that?" demanded Rianna. "Or were you listening?"

"Rianna! How could you say such a thing? Duncan said you were the hardest girl he'd ever known."

"I doubt it. I think he's had quite a lot of experience with all kinds of girls."

"But he's terribly fond of you, Rianna. You don't appreciate him." Lynda's voice took on a mournful note. "If only –" she stopped speaking and sighed, leaving her unfinished sentence hanging tantalisingly in the air.

"I must go in," Rianna began to walk towards the french windows of the villa.

"That photograph you took of Enrico and me –" Lynda had followed Rianna. "Will you let me have a print when it's ready?"

Rianna smiled coolly. "You can have the negative, too, if you really want it – if it's so important to you."

"Oh, yes, that would be best," agreed Lynda happily.

In the bedroom allocated to her for tonight, Rianna laughed aloud at her reflection in the mirror. Lynda was evidently scared of someone seeing a photograph of herself together with Enrico. Why? She need have no fear, for Rianna had not operated the camera, only pretending to click the shutter. But she was not disposed to let Lynda know that secret yet.

Next morning when the party set off for Selinunte and Agrigento, Rianna had half expected that Lynda would insist on joining, but she waved goodbyes as the three women, Emilia, Signora Cavallini and Rianna settled themselves in the car. The surprise, to Rianna, was that Enrico was to drive instead of one of the household chauffeurs.

She wondered if this was one of Emilia's subtle methods of choosing her own escort while suitably chaperoned by her mother.

But any minor elements of pairing relationships were forgotten when Rianna came to Selinunte, after not much more than an hour's run. The sight of the Greek temples, the gigantic ruins standing desolate against sea and sky, brought a sharp awareness of the superb architectural legacy those ancient people had left behind.

Emilia knew her history of the island and proved a competent guide. "The inhabitants of this most beautiful city were destroyed by the Carthaginians," she told Rianna. "Those who survived were taken to our own town of Marsala, which, as you know, was Lilybaeum."

"And the city was never rebuilt," murmured Rianna, gazing in wonderment at the Doric pillars of golden stone, the blocks lying in heaps on the ground.

"Some of these places have been restored," explained Emilia, "for after the destruction and then many years later, an earthquake, the whole place was forgotten. But this temple before us, the Temple of Juno, has been restored to the state it is believed to have been in about 500 B.C."

Rianna was busy with her cameras, using the ciné camera for the shots that required movement and a sense of approach and the smaller one for the carefully posed angles that lit the lovely columns and conveyed the poetry of the scene.

Signora Cavallini chose to remain in the car, but Emilia, Enrico and Rianna walked along the streets excavated only a few years ago, straight and geometrical. Flowers and grasses, oleanders and campanulas carpeted the spaces between the vestiges of columns and foundations of buildings and a flight of steps led to another temple with twelve re-erected columns, believed to be the original Acropolis.

"It will take me years to explore this island," murmured Rianna.

"When you see Agrigento, you will understand that in Sicily we are proud of our Greek heritage," replied Emilia.

In Sciacca Enrico suggested they might stop for lunch and see something of the town famous as a natural spa.

"I expect the Romans discovered the health waters," Rianna said. "They usually did, even in Britain."

"If we go down to the shore, it might be that the yacht *Celestina* would be in harbour," put in Emilia.

"That depends on how fast they're making the journey," returned Rianna, but she could not suppress the sense of eager anticipation that the sight of the yacht would arouse in her. She had to remind herself that it was Emilia also, who might be equally eager to see certain members of the crew.

At lunch in a restaurant on the waterfront Enrico said, "The best way to see Sciacca is from the sea, especially at night. Then you can see the buildings rise in tiers until they reach the castles."

"Oh, yes, the castles," put in Emilia. "Have we time to visit the enchanted castle?"

Enrico smiled. "One must always make time to visit enchanted castles." The tender glance he gave Emilia was not lost on

Rianna. Perhaps it was to be Enrico, this handsome Italian, who would marry Emilia, if she consented. Hope rose again in Rianna, but of course Holford might still be eager to claim Emilia – unless his responsibilities towards Lynda proved too heavy.

The enchanted castle proved to be a fascinating sight, for sculptured heads lay in masses on the ground, as though hundreds of statues had been summarily beheaded. Some heads had been set on small plinths perhaps a foot high on the ground, but this only made them look as though the rest of the figures were buried up to the shoulders.

"Oh, I can make an amusing story about these," Rianna exclaimed with enthusiasm. "What anecdotes these heads will tell!"

As Emilia had promised, Agrigento was a revelation. When the party arrived in the evening at the hotel which Emilia had booked, Rianna was surprised to find the town looking much like any other Sicilian town, with a railway station, squares and a wide avenue of trees leading to the outskirts. It was not until next day when Enrico drove the car to the "Valley of Temples" that Rianna saw that the "new city" although many centuries old, was built higher on an escarpment. It was an added attraction to find the various temples dotted about at some distance from each other, yet harmonising into a dramatic whole.

"In February," Emilia explained, "this whole area is covered with almond blossom and there is a special festival in the temples."

"Then next year I shall have to come here in February," replied Rianna. Between the temples were patches of wild flowers, mallow and convolvulus and red clover. She paused at one point to photograph a tree with mauve flowers and little tomato-like fruits all borne at the same time.

"It's a Falernum tree," explained Enrico, who was knowledgeable about plants, it seemed.

"I shall run out of film soon," Rianna complained with a laugh. "So much to photograph."

"Then save some for the temple of Zeus," advised Emilia.

"It's the largest in Sicily."

Rianna had read that originally this temple had giants twenty-four feet high upholding the roof supports, and now she was able to see one of the reconstructed figures lying on the ground close by. The stone was a deep pinkish red and the arms in the position of a figure supporting a great weight above his head. It was easy to visualise such giants in their original positions.

By the end of the day Rianna needed a respite from a surfeit of archaeological wonders, but Emilia was happily planning the next day for a visit to the beautiful museum.

"There you will see handsome Greek pottery, including the famous Gela vase, which was found there. It is very beautiful — black, with red decorations."

And, of course, a visit to the museum was not to be missed, but by next morning Rianna had rediscovered her youthful energy and was ready to appreciate the superb layout of this modern museum with its sculptures and pottery.

The party spent the next night in Gela by the coast before making the detour inland to Piazza Armerina, where the Roman villa at Casale had been excavated only in the last twenty years or so, to show the lovely mosaics.

"Nowhere else in the world," whispered Emilia, "is there now such a large collection so well preserved."

Rianna stood delighted at the scenes, not only the classical designs, but the portrayal of homely, everyday incidents; the small boy driving a chariot drawn by two indignant-looking ducks, a father chastising his small son with a whip, and of course the famous girls in their bikinis and performing games and physical exercises.

"And we thought we invented the bikini in the twentieth century," Rianna murmured to Emilia. "Oh, I could stay here day after day."

"Then you must come again for other visits," replied Emilia.

The party walked among the many new mosaics that were being uncovered during excavations, these roofed over with glass like greenhouses to protect them from damage by weather.

Today Rianna was given her first sight of Mount Etna, the

white cone and wide sloping shoulders dominating a large part of the island. It gave an illusion of floating in the luminous blue sky unharnessed to the land, as though it might vanish like a mirage. Rianna would never forget that first glimpse of the volcano, today bland and innocuous, but at any moment likely to erupt into flame and pour a mass of burning lava down the mountain slopes, destroying everything in its path.

"The name 'Etna' means the burning mountain," explained Emilia. "Two years ago we saw it lighting up the whole island at night and causing much damage. Now it is quiet again."

Rianna was slightly reluctant to leave this spot which commanded such a dazzling view, but as the others pointed out, there would be many more opportunities of viewing Etna from many angles all along the south and east coast of Sicily.

Enrico drove skilfully along the winding road into Syracuse and the landscape had changed from the long leafy avenues around Piazza Armerina to the light grey honeycombed limestone along the approaches to Syracuse.

'Do you think the *Celestina* will have arrived yet?" Rianna asked Emilia casually.

"One cannot tell. Perhaps they take a long time to make many dives on the way."

After dinner at the hotel on the Corso Gelone, Rianna accompanied Emilia and Enrico for a walk down to the harbour. A long causeway joined the newer section of the town to the older part, almost an island, with harbours on either side.

"Tomorrow we shall visit the cathedral and the museums and you'll see the fountain of Arethusa," promised Emilia.

Enrico had already discovered from a telephone call to the harbour authorities that the *Celestina* had not yet arrived. So Rianna curbed her impatience to meet the crew again. Naturally she wanted to hear how Martin had progressed, but that of course was pure self-deception, for she was aching to see Holford again, even though his attention would almost certainly be centred on Emilia.

CHAPTER NINE

ALMOST before she had finished her breakfast next morning, Rianna received two items of news. Emilia called to Rianna from the adjacent balcony to announce that the *Celestina* had reached harbour in Syracuse.

"And Holford has found a wrecked ship," she said eagerly. "Oh, I am so pleased for his success."

The Sicilian girl's animated face gave ample evidence to Rianna that Holford's triumph meant a great deal to her.

"I'm glad, too, that he's been fortunate," returned Rianna. "This is probably lucky for my brother as well."

"Ah, yes, it will be a feather in Martin's cap perhaps."

"I hope so." After a moment, Rianna asked, "Do you know if it's an ancient ship, the wreck, or something more modern?"

"No. Duncan did not know the details."

"Duncan? Is he here?" queried Rianna.

"Yes. He came last night – with Lynda."

This second item of news took Rianna by surprise, although after reflection she realised that she should have expected the arrival of Duncan and Lynda within the next day or two. Duncan, in any case, was bound to meet the yacht at Syracuse and Lynda would certainly not stay alone in the Cavallini villa, no matter how luxurious the surroundings.

Lynda was in the foyer of the hotel when Rianna saw her talking to Enrico.

"Oh, Rianna!" greeted Lynda. "You've arrived here, then."

"As you see. You're up early, aren't you?"

"I'm dead tired really with all the travelling and scarcely any sleep last night, but I couldn't wait when I heard the exciting

156

news. Do you think they will have found any real treasures?"

Rianna laughed. "I think that's unlikely, but any old piece of timber or an old cannon will please Holford and his crew."

"Much nicer if they could find a casket of jewels or gold coins," Lynda said.

"If they did, it would all go to the Italian government," put in Enrico.

"Really? How unfair!" Lynda made a little grimace, then turned her attention again to Enrico.

Rianna drifted away and went out into the street, only to run almost immediately into Duncan.

"Has the *Celestina* actually tied up in harbour?" she asked.

He nodded. "First, Holford has to report to the authorities about his find and get his permit for exploring the wreck."

"Is it ancient or modern?"

"Well, it's not a Roman galley. Holford thinks it might be part of a warship, sixteenth or seventeenth century."

"You've seen him this morning?" queried Rianna.

Duncan gazed down at her and smiled. "If you'd been up early enough, you could have come with me down to the harbour and given him the full treatment of that look in your eyes."

Rianna was angry with herself for again revealing to Duncan her secret preference for Holford and now turned her head away.

"I was forced to make do with Lynda's company on the way here," Duncan continued in a teasing voice. "You'd already spurned me, so there was nothing else for it."

"At least you had feminine company," she retorted lightly.

"But I would have chosen someone different – if I'd been allowed."

She laughed, for now she had regained her composure. "It's too early in the day to try flirting with me, Duncan. Surely you've some work to do."

For answer he took her arm and marched her towards the narrow neck of land that joined the peninsula. "Not even you can bother about work today. There's a celebration party on the yacht this evening, and I warn you now that I shall refuse to allow you to be monopolised by our host."

There was little chance of that, thought Rianna ruefully. With both Emilia and Lynda in attendance, Holford would have no time to spare.

"And where are you taking me now?" she asked Duncan, as they crossed the Umberto bridge and turned right towards the Foro Italico.

"To the fountain of Arethusa, of course."

"Yes, I know the legend. She was pursued and escaped by being turned into a spring of fresh water."

Duncan glanced down at her again with a teasing expression in his eyes. "I shall take precautions to see that you don't disappear into a spray of water."

She made no reply, but reflected that perhaps it was an advantage to have Duncan's companionship without strings attached, at least on her part, to counterbalance the fluctuations caused by Holford's disturbing uncertainties of mood.

But her resigned frame of mind did not last long, for when she and Duncan stood by the balustrade of Arethusa's fountain watching the ducks as they swam in and out of the papyrus stems, some intuitive sense urged her to look up. On the other side of the small pool Holford leaned against the seaward side of the balcony.

Duncan was telling her about the legend and that girls in Greece threw flowers into the river Alpheus and the garlands were carried by the current here to the pool.

"They say that this is one of the few places in Europe where papyrus grows. In Egypt they made paper from it."

Rianna heard the words but was not taking in the meaning, for her gaze was riveted on Holford's face, his cold expression as he stood there, unsmiling, even glowering. She was now aware that Duncan's arm was around her waist and his other hand over her wrist.

She did not know how long a time elapsed while she and Holford stared at each other, but it seemed like an eternity before Duncan became aware that Rianna's attention was elsewhere.

"Oh, there's Holford!" he exclaimed, and waved a greeting. He and Rianna began to move around the circumference of the pool towards him, but Holford's period of arrested motion had ended, for with a curt nod to Duncan and Rianna, he walked away smartly in the opposite direction.

Duncan began to laugh. "Well, really! I do believe I've upset the chief's apple-cart for once. How many more girls does he think he can string along? Surely he can't expect to monopolise them all. Let him be content with Emilia – and remember that there's always Lynda in the background waiting for the kill."

Duncan's choice of words again irritated Rianna. That phrase "waiting for the kill" hurt her more than Duncan could ever realise, for she knew now that Holford's heart had never been given to Lynda and that if he found himself forced to marry her, he would never find the happiness that Rianna hoped would be his, even if she were never the one to share it with him.

She allowed Duncan to show her some of the other important sites of Syracuse, the Cathedral which had originally been a temple to Minerva, one of the museums where the statues were painted in flesh colours. Now, if only for the sake of appearances, she tried to show some interest in his efforts to entertain her, but her thoughts had winged away to Holford.

Eventually she suggested that she must do more intensive work on filming the sights. "I shall bring my ciné camera this afternoon."

"Good. I'll be clapper-boy for you as well as porter," he offered.

Martin had arrived at the hotel by the time Rianna and Duncan returned for lunch.

"Did everything go well with you?" she asked her brother.

"On the whole, yes. The wreck is interesting, Holford thinks. We're all hoping that parts of it will remain in the same place by the time we get the permits from the Italian authorities. The sea has a habit of moving wreckage about and covering it up. We've left a marker buoy, so we're hoping for the best."

"Supposing someone else finds your marker buoy and decides to explore?" she suggested.

"We can't exactly prevent that, but Holford would have some harsh words to say to somebody if that happened."

"I hear there's to be a celebration 'do' on the yacht tonight. Correct?"

"Oh, yes. I was going to tell you. Done any filming this morning?"

"No, only some shots with the little camera."

"Then we'll go together this afternoon and do the archaeological part – the Greek theatre and so on."

Rianna collected her equipment after lunch and was glad to escape quickly in a taxi with Martin, before Duncan could attach himself to her.

"The Greek theatre first, I think," suggested Martin, "while we have the light in the right direction. Then after the Roman amphitheatre, we'll do those caves and grottoes and listen to the echo in Dionysius' ear, as they say."

It was relaxing, thought Rianna, to be with her brother working in their accustomed way, checking the best view points for scenic value. Yet underneath Martin's efficient manner there was a certain tension as though part of his mind were occupied elsewhere.

In the cave where the ropemakers had twisted their ropes since the Middle Ages, she asked tentatively, "Anything worrying you Martin?"

"Perhaps," he answered, after a pause. "Did you come with Duncan from Marsala?"

"No. With Emilia and her mother and Enrico. Why?"

Martin's lips tightened. "Lynda has thrown out some subtle hints that you started out with the Cavallinis, but changed over to Duncan's car afterwards."

"How on earth can she maintain that outrageous lie!" demanded Rianna. "She and Duncan travelled together, so I understand. In any case, Holford – if it's Holford who's so concerned about me – can easily ask Emilia."

"I hate to sound unflattering," Martin grinned at her disarmingly, "but I think he's more concerned about Duncan than about you. First, as you know, Duncan opted out of this trip round the coast. It's true, he wasn't really quite fit, but all the same, it does look as though he wanted to travel overland, preferably with you."

"As a matter of fact, he offered. I refused his escort, because I'd already promised Emilia and let her make arrangements. Lynda was up at the Cavallini villa." Then a sudden thought struck Rianna. "Oh, of course! Now I think I see it clearly. She wanted to travel with Enrico, but she was denied that chance because he came with us and drove the car. So she probably asked Duncan to bring her here."

Rianna went on to tell Martin of the small episode in the Cavallini garden when she had only pretended to photograph Enrico with Lynda.

Martin laughed. "What a pity you didn't really take her in some compromising position with Enrico. Then you could blackmail her!"

"Perhaps that's what she's afraid of, though I don't know why."

"Well, anyway, I've warned you about her gossiping tongue, so you can be on your guard."

As they wandered about the orange groves and explored other caves, Rianna hardly knew whether to be elated or not by her brother's disclosure. Now she thought she understood the meaning of Holford's scowling expression when she and Duncan were at Arethusa's fountain. Yet could that possibly mean that he was jealous of Duncan? She repressed the unruly thought.

A party of people with their guide were visiting the cave of Dionysius' Ear and Martin and Rianna waited until they had drifted away. One or two stragglers were still trying to make their voices echo, after the guide had demonstrated the curious properties of the cave and explained how Dionysius had been able to listen to all that went on down below.

Then Rianna was startled to hear a voice singing "Duncan is my darling, my darling, my darling. Duncan is Rianna's favourite cavalier."

The echo rolled on . . . "cavalier . . . cavalier. . ."

The next moment she came face to face with Holford, followed by Lynda

"Trying the echoes?" Holford asked Rianna, his face slightly

161

twisted with distaste.

"No," she answered quickly. "I thought Lynda was doing just that."

"I?" Lynda's pretty face was a study in complete innocence. "I didn't hear anything. Did you, Holford?"

"I – well, it doesn't matter."

Rianna understood perfectly. Holford imagined that she had deliberately taken this opportunity of hammering home to him where her own inclinations lay. After all, in the sound distortion of voices echoing in a cave, how could he know which girl was singing the tune? She wondered if Lynda had already seen her and Martin, but realised that the point hardly mattered.

But Rianna was not inclined to accept defeat so easily, especially at the hands of Lynda. "Why don't we all try out the echo?" she suggested. "Lynda can show us the right place."

"Oh, no, thanks," replied Lynda hastily. "Listeners never hear any good of themselves, so they say." She shot a malicious glance at Rianna.

"But one doesn't have to make a whole speech," retorted Rianna. "Just a single word would do, or a name. Like Enrico, for instance. That should echo well."

In the dim light of the cavern Rianna could not see whether Lynda's face changed colour, but she was sure that her shot had gone home, for Lynda turned petulantly to Holford. "Oh, come on, Holford, we've seen enough of these gloomy places. Let's go."

Martin arrived then and wanted a film taken of Rianna walking just outside the cave, to give scale to the immense height, taller than some of the fully-grown trees close by.

In the evening it was Martin who took her aboard the *Celestina* lying out in the harbour. Holford had not even mentioned any kind of dinner-party or celebration. In the end the affair could scarcely be called a party or a celebration, since Holford was missing and so were Emilia and her mother and Enrico.

Jeffrey admitted that he had cheated over the cooking and had most of the dishes sent aboard from a restaurant.

"I simply hadn't time today with all my marine specimens to

attend to – and pickling my fishy creatures in formalin doesn't exactly mix with cooking."

Rianna laughed. "You never know, it might add a unique flavour to the spaghetti!"

Lynda was obviously disgruntled at the non-appearance of Holford. She had evidently not been aware of his intended absence.

"He should have been here," she said crossly. "After all, he's supposed to have something to celebrate."

"Perhaps he *is* celebrating somewhere, for all we know," put in Duncan with a mischievous glance at Lynda. "Wining and dining with Emilia and her companions."

"Lucky chap!" commented Martin. "No offence to you, Lynda."

"I suppose it doesn't matter if Rianna is offended," put in Duncan. "She's only your sister."

"That's right," agreed Rianna quickly, with a smile. "Sisters are used to such treatment."

After dinner, on the deck Rianna took the opportunity to talk with Steve, the medical member of the team.

"Tell me about the risks of underwater exploring," she suggested. "Holford seems anxious that I should at least make one venture to discover at first hand what it's like roaming about in the depths."

Steve smiled. "As long as you're fit and a good swimmer, you can't come to much harm, unless you're alone, and you must never be alone. We have to partner each other."

"And no alcohol before diving."

He nodded. "Nor, of course, a substantial meal. But you wouldn't swim in those conditions, anyway. Holford won't let you use the scuba method, you know. It'll have to be only snorkel. He makes it a rule that everyone in his team must be absolutely perfect in skin-diving with a snorkel before they attempt the scuba method with an air cylinder and all the rest."

She was trying to lead up to the question of Jack Patterson's tragedy, but could not yet find the right approach.

"My brother is very particular about conforming to all the

163

regulations," she said. "He feels he's responsible for recording all the hard work that other members put in and also he has to look after his expensive equipment, cameras and so on."

"Yes," agreed Steve, gazing across the water towards the opposite side of the bay where a purple-grey tongue of land jutted out against the deep twilight sky. Then he turned to face her. "I think you're really asking for my reassurance about your brother, because he's cameraman – and you know about Jack!" He glanced quickly at her. "You do know about Lynda's husband?"

"I've heard some of the details. Not much."

Steve sighed. "I'm afraid Jack had only himself to blame. He drank too much, for one thing, even if he avoided alcohol just before diving, but that's not enough. You have to be more sparing than that."

"What actually happened?" Rianna tried not to sound too eager, but she was memorising every word.

"Well, he committed one crime to start with. He went down alone and his absence wasn't noticed until probably half an hour after he'd gone over the side of the yacht. The depth there was about seventy feet, so he should have begun surfacing soon. Holford and Duncan went down immediately to search for him, but apparently he indicated by signs that he was O.K." Steve paused thoughtfully and lit a cigar. "After that, events became confused. Duncan surfaced in the ordinary way, so Holford was left with the responsibility. It seems then that Jack's air cylinder was exhausted, so he had to share Holford's."

"How could he do that?" queried Rianna.

"Easily. You pass the mouthpiece to your partner back and forth, but you must control your breathing, exhaling while you ascend, then inhaling, twice, and holding the second breath. Apparently somewhere on the ascent Jack lost consciousness and Holford had to bring him to the surface as quickly as possible, but not too quickly to cause damage to Jack's lungs." Steve paused again before resuming. "I knew when Jack was lifted aboard the yacht that he was probably gone. Everyone did their best – we radioed to the nearest land and we got him to the hospital in a very short time, but he was dead long before then."

"But Holford? It surely wasn't his fault?"

"Nothing was his fault, and he's a fool to go on blaming himself. Jack went down against all the rules. Apart from anything else, by the time Holford tried to rescue him, it was practically dark, and no one but a fool dives at night if he can help it."

"So actually Holford and Duncan were risking their own lives in trying to rescue Jack?"

Steve nodded. "Admitted, but you don't think of that kind of cost when you're trying to help one of your own men."

"Was there an inquiry?"

"Two in fact. One at a small local town off the west coast of Borneo and a second one at Singapore. Unfortunately, Holford refused to use the only piece of evidence that would have completely cleared him of responsibility. Jack left a letter in his cabin. It fell out of a pocket when I was collecting his personal belongings. It wasn't addressed to Holford or anyone else – and I read it. Apparently, Lynda wanted a divorce and Jack assumed she wanted to marry Holford, so – he took that way out."

"You mean – suicide?"

"It amounted to that – although he could easily have caused the deaths of others. I took the note to Holford and, like a fool, he destroyed it. He wouldn't have Lynda mixed up in such an affair, he said. Nor did he relish the fact that one of his team chose to end his own life."

When Steve fell silent, Rianna murmured a quiet, "Thank you for telling me this." Then she in her turn remained hushed, for she now realised even more strongly the clenching hold that Lynda could exercise over Holford. Without that revealing letter, he was powerless to oppose her.

"What are you two plotting?" Lynda's voice came from close by and Rianna wondered if the girl had been standing there for some time, listening to Steve's explanation.

"How we can throw you overboard and then make you reappear as a nymph on top of Arethusa's fountain," answered Steve in his lazy drawl.

Lynda shuddered exaggeratedly. "What a terrible fate! What have you in mind for Rianna, then?"

"Perhaps a gentle wafting through the air to land –"

"On the uncomfortable turrets and pinnacles of the Cathedral," finished Rianna for him.

In the dinghy going ashore, Lynda complained that the evening had been extraordinarily dull.

"How unflattering can you be!" grumbled Martin who had undertaken to escort the two girls ashore to their hotel.

"Well, I missed Holford," continued Lynda. "Where on earth was he?"

"Actually dining with a couple of influential men connected with the harbour authorities and the Italian government archaeological department that deals with underwater finds." It was Steve who spoke crisply.

"Then why couldn't you have said so in the first place?" Lynda was furious.

Steve grinned. "Frankly, dear Lynda, because I thought it more fun to keep you guessing."

"And you kept Rianna guessing, too!" declared Lynda.

Rianna shook her head. "No, indeed, I wasn't all that curious – or perturbed about Holford's absence."

"Naturally not. You had Duncan there – as always at your elbow," was Lynda's over-sweet reply.

Duncan and Jeffrey had stayed aboard the yacht, for they could not leave the ship with no one in charge, and, as usual, Carlo, the navigator, was ashore with his friends.

At the hotel when Martin delivered the two girls, Rianna was handed a note at the reception desk.

As she hastily read the few lines, she whispered to Martin, "It's from Emilia – they've gone – unexpectedly, she says. To Palermo. She's sorry about not staying here longer."

Martin whistled softly. "Now I wonder why they've all hared off like that in such a hurry."

"Business matters, perhaps."

"But the business is in Marsala, not Palermo," he pointed out.

"True. I'll tell Lynda and put her out of her misery thinking that Holford is gadding around somewhere with Emilia after he's finished with his men companions."

Lynda's eyes gleamed with something like triumph when Rianna gave her the news, but almost immediately she veiled her eyes and turned away. It was not until the next day that Rianna understood the meaning of that exultant glance.

She accompanied Martin to the museum to view the exquisite coins for which Syracuse was renowned, although some had been found at Selinunte and the early specimens bore the celery leaf emblem from which Selinunte had taken its name.

The routine of viewing the coins was impressive, for not more than twelve people were allowed into the strongroom at a time, and then firmly locked in.

"So that we can't decamp with the loot," whispered Martin.

Rianna was lost in wonderment at the delicacy of the engraving of the coins, gold pieces no more than an inch in diameter and sometimes less, inscribed with the heads of gods or goddesses. One was of the nymph Arethusa, surrounded by dolphins, and on the reverse a galloping quadriga surmounted by a winged victory.

"It's amazing that anyone could fashion a coin in such minute detail," murmured Rianna. "Look at those four horses, every leg is there, beautifully exact."

"They knew their job, those old artists, and did all their work without the modern aids we know now."

Rianna looked up startled to find Holford next to her apparently engrossed in examining one of the coins in the glass case.

"They had to make their own cutting tools," he continued, apparently unaware of her presence or, at least, he was pretending to ignore her. "It's doubtful if they had any kind of magnifying lens."

"All they had was their own perfect eyesight," chipped in Rianna. Now he stood up to look at her and smiled. His sleeve brushed her arm and she could certainly not pretend that his presence so close to her did not affect her.

"I didn't expect to see you here this morning," she said lamely, kicking herself because she could think of nothing more illuminating to say.

"Why? Did you think I was out on the town carousing last night?"

"You might have been," she replied. "Were you?"

"What would the rest of the boys say if that were true?" Then, as he noted that Martin was engaged at an opposite showcase, he said quietly and with a distinct change of manner, "Duncan not accompanying you – as usual?"

"No," she snapped. "Perhaps he has more important work to do than escort me – *as usual.*"

The time limit for viewing the coins was reached and the party of a dozen people was ushered out into the adjoining room and thence into a corridor.

Holford remained by her side as they paced one of the galleries with superb sculptures.

After a few minutes Martin joined them, saying that he had secured a permit to photograph some of the sculptures when that part of the museum was closed to the public.

"So you'd better write up all the details, Rianna," he instructed her.

She imagined that Holford would quietly drift away when she adopted the businesslike method of taking out her notebook and pen, but instead he dictated to her particulars of each statue or decorative piece of marble.

"I shall have to come back later," Martin decided, "and bring my own lighting."

So the three walked out into the courtyard and down through the shady archway to the Arethusa fountain. Martin went away some distance in order to focus certain shots of the arch and Rianna was about to join him when Holford laid a restraining hand on her wrist, a gesture that did nothing to calm her hot resentment, but merely added fire to her veins. Oh, why must he torment her in this way?

"Rianna, I want to know something and I want the truth," he began bluntly enough. "Are you in love with Duncan?"

She had not been prepared for quite so direct a question, but she found strength to answer as directly, "Is it your business if I am?"

168

"Yes, it is," he snapped, and his blue eyes seemed to flash fire. "I understand that you made an arrangement to travel with him to Syracuse."

"Who told you that?" she demanded in a low, furious whisper.

"I wish Duncan had been more honest with me at the start," he went on, ignoring her question. "He need not have made an excuse not to sail with us."

"That was nothing to do with me. He had a cold – and you, of all people, know the rules about absolute fitness."

He smiled with derision. "Is that what he told you? And did he have a cold? The excuse he gave me was quite different. He said you'd asked him to be your escort on the trip from Marsala, so that he could point out the places of interest for your films."

So much rage welled up in Rianna that she found it difficult not to raise her hand and slap it hard against his face.

"Obviously, there's nothing I can say that will make you believe what you don't want to believe. Duncan offered, yes, and I refused. I came all the way with Emilia and her mother with Enrico driving. Ask them, if you really want to know the truth."

"You know quite well that I can't ask them. Emilia is in Palermo for a singing audition. Her father is opposed to any kind of career for her and that of a singer would be a family disgrace. Lynda assures me that she was the one who came in the car with the Cavallinis and you accompanied Duncan in his car."

She glared at him, but this time he did not meet her glance. "And stayed with him at the various hotels en route? Why don't you check all those hotels and make sure that I shared Duncan's room every time?"

Now suddenly Rianna knew the meaning of Lynda's victorious expression when she learned of Emilia's departure. There was no one to corroborate Rianna's version of her own journey. Well, not yet, she thought, but sooner or later, she would hammer the truth into Holford. She would make him eat his words. She would make him take back all his insinuations. She would –

Holford was speaking and at first the words did not register, but gradually she found herself listening. ". . . I wish I'd known from the start that it was Duncan who attracted you. I know I ought to have seen it coming. But I was a fool, ten times a fool. For I found that I'd fallen in love with you – and if I'd had the slightest hope that you cared in the least for me, then I'd have sent Lynda packing. She's a stronger creature than she appears, but together we could have fought her. I'm sorry, Rianna, but I won't trouble you again. Let's forget this morning ever happened."

He had walked away with brisk, decisive steps and had vanished up a narrow street while she stood rooted to the ground, longing to run after him, beg him to say it all over again.

Oh, why had she let her rebellious tongue run away with her? Of course he had wanted to know if she loved Duncan, but she could have told him seriously and quietly that she did not. No, she had to flare up and fling phrases in his face, phrases that had no meaning for herself, but would take on a disastrous significance for Holford.

Martin rejoined her, making some conventional remark about a particular series of films he had taken.

"You look as if you've seen a ghost. Where's Holford?"

"Gone." The word rang in her mind like a tolling bell. She felt hollow inside, drained now of emotion, aware only that the ghost she had seen was that of a lost love. Perhaps not even lost, but wantonly thrown away.

CHAPTER TEN

RIANNA was engrossed in typing articles when Martin came for a week-end visit to the Casa Rosa in Marsala. She had returned there immediately from Syracuse and since then in the last eight weeks or so had driven the small car over many parts of the island, filming and photographing sights and scenes that appealed to her. She had travelled to some of the lesser-known villages in the centre of the island, seeking the out-of-the-way corners where few tourists ever penetrated.

"What's the news?" Martin asked, flopping into a chair.

"Not bad. Several travel articles accepted for next year's brochures. That piece I did about the Cavallini wine establishment – that's going into a series of 'Wines of the World'. A couple of television producers are interested in anything we can do that's not quite so well known – and I've plenty of material."

Martin smiled "Smart girl! You've done well. Our bank balance is rather shaky, so we can do with some bolstering up."

"Oh, yes. A county education authority might want one of our films of the Greek and Roman antiquities if we can add an interesting commentary dealing with the history of the sites. I've already done most of that, but might have a few references to look up later."

"And besides all this work, what have you been doing with yourself in the way of amusement?" Martin grinned at her.

"Oh, I've found most of that driving about from one place to another. I've been up to the Cavallini villa a couple of times by invitation for dinner or to spend a day there and swim in their pool. By the way, I suppose you know –" She broke off and glanced questioningly at her brother.

171

"That Emilia and Enrico are engaged? Oh, yes, the news filtered aboard the yacht. I don't know what Holford's reactions were, but I suppose he wasn't all that serious about her."

"Any more than you were?"

Martin laughed. "Well, I don't know. If I'd thought there was a slim chance coming my way, I might have grabbed it. But the Emilias of this world don't hang about for chaps like me."

"And Emilia has been accepted for a certain amount of training as a singer, she tells me," continued Rianna. "Her father would always have opposed such a revolutionary notion, but it seems that Enrico will encourage her to sing at recitals and perhaps concerts."

"A pity to waste a glorious voice," commented Martin. "She'd make a wonderful Tosca or a Carmen."

"Have you seen anything of Lynda lately? I suppose she is still at Syracuse?"

"She seems to have struck up an acquaintance with an American staying in the hotel. How long that will last is anyone's guess, but at least she isn't flittering around us and making a nuisance of herself." After a pause, he said slyly, "You haven't asked about Duncan."

"I just assume he's busy along with the rest of you."

"And Holford?"

"No doubt he, too, is well occupied with directing the diving schedules. Have you found any more of the wreck?"

"Yes. Enough to identify that she might be a ship of about the 1550s, armed, of course, It was a wonderful phrase, she reflected, found have been everyday articles, like plates and dishes, usually pewter, knives, a sword or two, and a lovely pepper-pot, used no doubt at the captain's table."

Rianna put aside her work to spend the evening with Martin at one of the hotels in the centre of Marsala. He chose the Hotel Bolzano and Rianna could have preferred any other hotel in the whole of Sicily, for the Bolzano was where she and Martin had first met Holford.

During the last couple of months she had concentrated on her work, striving to forget the man to whom she had so foolishly given her heart, and she was proud of the fact that by now she had accomplished a great part of what she and her brother had set out to achieve. Those first few weeks had been wasted as far as tangible results were concerned, but the effect on her life had been devastating.

She turned her thoughts away from Holford, although her next remark was still connected with him. "It was a waste of money renting that Villa Aurelia. None of you used it much."

"Perhaps Holford took it for Lynda's sake, so that she would have somewhere comfortable."

Rianna laughed. "Comfortable, yes, but not very interesting when all the men had flown. How could he have expected her to stay there just with the housekeeper?"

"I expect he knows her ways by now." Martin's expression changed to one of perplexity. "I've never understood why he tolerated her, a querulous little creature like that. I know she's Jack's widow, but that marriage was breaking up anyway, so I'm told."

"Then let's all hope her American friend occupies her for a while longer," suggested Rianna lightly. Her spirits were the reverse of buoyant, though, for she now realised with a sickening certainty that the opposition of her rivals, or fancied rivals, had vanished. With Emilia engaged and Lynda at least temporarily occupied, the way would have been clear for Rianna had she not thrown insuperable obstacles in the way.

Much as she loved her brother, she was relieved when he left next day to return to Syracuse. He was too poignant a reminder of his connection with Holford. No doubt when they were back in England, the memory would fade and she would recover completely that happy affinity which had always existed between them.

When she went into her bedroom after seeing him off in the car he had hired from Syracuse, her glance fell on an untidily-wrapped parcel on her dressing-table. Inside was a large piece of pink coral branching delicately from a central core.

How good of Martin to bring her such a gift, she thought.

Then she saw the note folded so small that she almost threw it away with the wrappings.

"A present from Syracuse. Holford hopes you can make use of it for a necklace or something."

The handwriting was Martin's, so was she now to understand that the gift was from Holford? A peace-offering? A farewell trifle from the sea?

She stared at the lovely twisting shapes, the way the light caught the pink colours, and her eyes filled with tears. Angry with herself, she brushed away those useless tears and decided to photograph the coral against a dark green background. It was easy enough to close the shutters and obscure the daylight and she tried several positions as well as two or three different backgrounds.

If only she could turn every sentimental object to some practical use, she reflected, then life would be much easier.

Yet her thoughts would not be diverted from Holford. She recalled his words that night he came to the Casa Rosa when he had mentioned another girl – "but she's otherwise engaged". At the time she had assumed he meant Emilia. Now she wondered if he had indicated herself. She had told him, impressed upon him in fact, that she had come to Sicily to work on her projects and had no time to dally. But then she smiled. Men of the calibre of Holford were not so easily repelled as that by the mere mention of one's life work.

She realised now that Duncan had not been a true friend. He had probably wanted no more than a pleasant spell of philandering, but she need not have allowed him to push her into an impossible position with regard to Holford.

At the end of the week a letter came from Martin, suggesting that she might go to Syracuse for a special performance of ballet in the Greek theatre.

Rianna had already visited several festivals and entertainments held in different provinces during the summer, including the Sicilian Cart and Costume rally at Taormina, and open-air opera at Trapani. But she had carefully refrained from going to Syra-

174

cuse for the most obvious reasons. She hardly wanted to run into Holford or Duncan or any of the others.

She consulted the long diary of summer events all over the island. Most of the performances at Syracuse took place during June and July, so as this was now late August, it must be an extra show.

Although the new motorways made it possible to reach Syracuse in one day, Rianna decided to make a detour via Enna, stay the night there and film whatever took her fancy. She found so much of interest in the city that she regretted not giving herself more time, but promised that she would make another visit later.

"The belvedere of Sicily," the hotel proprietor informed her, and he was undoubtedly right, for the city stood some three thousand feet above sea level and from different vantage points commanded a view of almost the whole of the island. Away to the east was the mauve-blue cone of Etna, shimmering on the skyline as though floating above the earth. In the other directions there were the long ranges of mountains running down to Syracuse or north-west to Palermo.

The town had some strange troglodyte houses and Rianna was lucky enough to find several of the inhabitants willing to pose outside their dwellings and afterwards invite her inside to look at their homes.

Elsewhere, there were castles and palaces of interest, but most of all, Rianna was fascinated by the fact that many of the women wore magnificent black shawls called *mantelline*. Eventually she found a shop where such shawls were on sale and by now her Italian was reaonably good enough to ask the shopkeeper something about her wares. Rianna learned that each town or district favoured a particular kind of border or fringe. In Enna, the fringe was usually black, though the woman had some shawls where the fringe was half black and half white. Rianna bought one of those.

"But the custom dies, *signorina*," lamented the shopkeeper. "When I was young, everyone in country places wore the shawl. Now only in the mountains."

The road from Enna through the mountains to Syracuse twisted and turned like a wriggling eel and there were times when Rianna almost wished that she had chosen the other route to Catania and then taken the coast motorway, but this way was much more interesting, for new vistas opened out with every turn of the road. She even began to sing to herself. Let those who want motorways travel on them!

It was late when she eventually arrived at Syracuse and met Martin at the hotel.

"I thought you weren't coming," he said.

"I took my time – and did some interesting work on the way. What's exciting about this ballet here?"

"It's a company from Naples, but also there's a sea festival tomorrow, boat races in front of the Marina, fireworks – all the trimmings that Italians can provide to these *festas.*"

"Are you the only one ashore?" she queried. "Everyone else on the yacht?"

Martin grinned at her. "And whom particularly were you expecting to welcome you? Duncan? Holford? Sorry I'm a mere brother."

He took her out to a restaurant for a late supper, ordered some wine and raised his glass to her. "You won't be pestered by Lynda this time. She's gone off on a yachting trip with her American and some of his friends."

"A bigger and better yacht than the *Celestina,* I hope," she commented, but the news was welcome.

She spent part of the next day in her hotel room, writing up the notes of Enna and other places. The boat races were to begin at six o'clock and she was ready when Martin called for her. They met Jeffrey along the promenade and he guided the others to a spot from which all the races could be seen in the Grand Harbour.

Rianna perched herself on a flat-topped wall and had her camera at the ready. Few of the races were meant to be taken seriously, for the crews, often dressed in sixteenth-century costume, were not so enthusiastic about winning the event as ducking their opponents in the water. At times the harbour was a confused kaleidoscope of colour and movement, mingling with shrill laughter, the sound of mandolins and guitars or a raucous radio.

The fireworks were spectacular, as always in Mediterranean countries, multi-coloured rockets and stars exploding into bouquets of flowers or dazzling rain, and Rianna clapped her hands in delight.

When Martin announced that he was starving and needed dinner to prevent him from collapsing through hunger, she accompanied the two men to the hotel.

"But the ballet performance?" she remembered suddenly. "Have we missed it?"

"No," answered Martin. "The company postponed their performance until tomorrow. They didn't want to compete with a sea festival, they said."

"Very wise of them," agreed Rianna.

Next evening the Greek theatre arena was almost full when Rianna and Martin arrived.

"Isn't this a good way of using an ancient treasure!" she commented. "To perform here as actors did more than a couple of thousand years ago. The architect chose a wonderful spot. You can see all the city from here and the sea as well."

"I'm told that at one time the Greek citizens crowded here to watch real naval battles," Martin told her. "And no doubt the suspense was greater than any drama, for on the result depended their fate – slavery, slaughter and all the rest."

The first ballet to be performed was Stravinsky's *Apollo*, and as the twilight deepened and subtle lighting came into play, Rianna could easily imagine that she had been transported back into time and was actually watching a vision of Apollo himself inspiring the three Muses. After Calliope danced her variation, Rianna stood up to allow several members of the audience to pass to their seats and she was utterly surprised, perhaps even dismayed, when she saw that one of them was Holford. After some shuffling he was sitting next to her and the smile he gave her as the stage-lighting caught his face almost intoxicated her.

"Sorry to be late," he whispered, but there was no time for

further explanations, for the next variation, that of the muse Polyhymnia, symbolising mime and rhetoric, had begun. Rianna's attention was riveted on to the dancer, but she could hear own heart beating like a mad thing.

In the next short interval she searched for some harmless topic of conversation. "Thank you for the piece of coral," she murmured.

He turned towards her, but this time she could not see his eyes. "I'm glad you didn't send it back."

"Send it back?" she echoed, but again there was no time for further explanations.

She had to wait until there was another pause before the coda when Apollo danced with all three Muses, including the third, Terpsichore.

"Why should I send back the coral? Didn't you mean it for me?"

"I told Martin that if you decided not to accept it, he was to bring it back to me."

She was silent for a while digesting this instruction, which of course Martin had never fulfilled. But should she tell Holford that?

"Did you mean then – that –" she broke off, twisting her thoughts into a shape that she hardly dared put into words. "That if I rejected the coral – then I would be –?"

"Naturally. I thought it was faint-hearted not to have one more try, pugnacious, hot-tempered girl that you are."

"I was glad to keep it," she whispered, still trying to restrain that soaring elation that would not be repressed. His hand closed over hers and the dancing had begun again. At first she was too excited to concentrate on watching the spectacle she had come to see, but gradually a calmness seemed to flow into her from his touch.

At the end of *Apollo* and after the interval there would be another short ballet based on Ariadne, but Holford guided Rianna to the topmost level of the huge arena.

"There will be other times when we can watch ballet in a Greek theatre," he said. "This moment will never come again,

178

my love, my darling Rianna." In the darkness against the background of trees and in the shadow of an ancient wall, she melted into his arms while he kissed her with passionate tenderness and whispered endearments that sounded to Rianna like the honeyed words of paradise.

"Perhaps a long time ago other people came here in the darkness," she said, "and whispered loving words to each other."

He jerked her slightly away from him. "I've said my piece," he declared. "I've confessed that I love you, that I fell for you almost from that first day when you came with your brother. But I'm still listening for any like admission on your part."

She laughed and clung to him, her head on his shoulder. "Do you really need to be told in words of one syllable?"

"Yes."

"Isn't the coral enough?"

"No," he snapped. "I want to hear the right words – never mind the coral."

"Holford, how blind could you be? I was so determined not to be the kind of girl who hangs around for casual flirtations that I'm afraid I overdid the part. You see, I thought at one time you were – sort of – bound to Lynda."

"Only in her estimation – and that's all finished now."

"Then I thought the beautiful Emilia was your attraction."

"Hold on!" he exclaimed. "You don't have much of an opinion of me – one girl after another."

"Does it matter what opinion I have of you if I love you?" she countered.

"Ah, that's better. Now you've said it."

They remained locked in close embrace until a wave of applause reached them from the arena below. Because they were in no hurry to leave this enchanted place, Holford dawdled towards the spot where he had left his car.

"I'm still puzzled about Emilia," she said. "Why did she leave so hurriedly for Palermo? Didn't she know about the audition?"

Holford laughed. "Well, I think she knew, but to appease her father, she made a trip to Syracuse as a sort of blind."

"Like going up to Birmingham by way of Beachy Head?"

"That's it. But her father has become more reconciled to the idea that she might sing in public for pleasure, if not for a living."

"I'm glad about that. She has too beautiful a voice to allow it to rust." After a pause, she added, "I wonder if Martin is looking for me."

"He's probably gone back to the city long ago – like a good brother. Actually, you can thank him some time for his help."

"In what way?"

"Well, he assured me that you were certainly not involved with Duncan – and you must forgive me for those accusations, but I was mad to see you on such friendly terms with him. And Martin hinted that if I went the right way about it, I might induce you to drop that working-girl attitude – leave-me-alone-I'm-here-to-film-Sicily idea – and spare a thought for love."

"I'm glad to hear that brothers can be useful sometimes," she said gaily. "I realize now what you meant that night when you spoke of being drawn to a girl who was otherwise engaged. But I thought you meant either Emilia – or perhaps a girl at home in England, or even elsewhere."

"Idiot!" he growled, pulling her into his arms.

It was long past midnight when they returned to the hotel, but Martin was patiently waiting in the foyer.

He looked at each of them in turn and muttered, "About time, too! Good-night, the pair of you. You don't need me."

But he paused long enough to kiss his sister and shake Holford's hand before he went quickly towards the outer door, and into the street.

"Have you to go back to the yacht?" Rianna asked Holford.

"Yes, with Martin. But the *Celestina* is not far out. We have the dinghy."

Suddenly she became contrite. "In all this excitement, I've forgotten to ask about your work – the wreck and the finds you've made."

"Time for that tomorrow. The whole project has gone very well. We've been able to fish up several objects that the Italian

180

museums are glad to have. Good-night, darling. Much as I hate to leave you now, I can't keep Martin waiting any longer."

In her room Rianna moved about, unable to settle to do anything at all out of pure exultation. Her heart was singing the song that only requited love knows. When at last she slipped into bed she fell into a rapturous dream where she was dancing on the stage of the Greek theatre and Holford was her Apollo, seeking her out and rejecting the other two Muses.

She was idling next morning in the hotel garden when a waiter brought her a telephone message. Would she come at once down to the harbour where the motor dinghy would be waiting?

Unknown fears clamoured at her consciousness all the way in a taxi down to the harbour, for she had not waited to take her car from the garage. Duncan was there, his face more grave than she had ever seen it.

"What is it?" Her face had whitened as the blood drained away.

"A slight accident, but we think it will be all right."

"Holford? Or Martin?" '

"Both," he answered tersely, as he started the motor dinghy towards the yacht.

"What sort of accident?" She prayed that this was not to be a repetition of the tragedy that had happened to Jack. Lynda's phrase came into her mind — "Holford always seems to be unlucky with his cameramen."

"It's at the wreck," replied Duncan. "Martin may be trapped inside part of the hull."

She swallowed a large obstruction in her throat, but she would not surrender to tears that could serve no useful purpose. "And Holford?"

"Is down there rescuing him. Jeffrey, as well."

She remained silent until Steve helped her aboard the *Celestina*. Duncan went down below to change into diving gear.

"Serious?" she asked Steve.

"Not yet. They can all be down there quite a while longer without any danger, but time is eventually important."

The yacht was now well outside the harbour and several marker buoys bobbed close by.

"Is it very deep just here?" she queried.

"No. About fifty feet, which means they have a margin of time before they need stop on the way for decompression. Martin has been down with Jeffrey for less than an hour, Holford went down only half an hour ago."

"But what's happened?" She tried not to sound impatient.

"Well, the sea never remains the same. It shifts about and that's why wrecks often become unmanageable. Sand or rocks move with the currents and I understand that a piece of timber has trapped Martin inside the hull. An accident that no one could foresee."

Duncan called to Steve for help in putting on his scuba suit and air cylinder and Rianna was left alone to wander the deck, idly noticing Jeffrey's specimens of marine creatures spread out in trays to dry.

After Duncan had descended the minutes ticked by and Rianna remained close to Steve who was attending to the signal line. It seemed like hours, but was no more than ten minutes by her watch when Steve muttered that someone was coming up.

Her breath was coming in gasps as she tried to control her nerves, stretched now almost to breaking point. Who would come up? In good health or on the point of death? Surely Fate could not be unkind as to snatch from her the two men she loved best. If she was to be deprived of one or other, which would be her impossible choice?

She knew she had no choice, for Holford had pointed out long ago that the sea was relentless and masterful and possessed overwhelming power.

The ascent was so slow that Rianna almost screamed with the tension. Steve said quietly, "Be patient, Rianna. Their safety depends on each man taking his own time. He mustn't come up too fast."

She calmed herself, but was hardly relieved when it was Jeffrey who surfaced first. Steve helped him on board.

"They're all right. Holford has been able to pull Martin out of the space between the timbers."

"Is Martin's air cylinder still functioning?" Steve queried anxiously.

"As far as I know. In any case the other two have fairly full cylinders." Jeffrey went down the deck, his fins flapping noisily. In one hand he swung a bucket of specimens and she watched him tip them into a tank of fresh water. How could a man dabble with starfish and other marine creatures when three of his own kind were so recently in danger and might yet not be wholly safe?

Then she realised that men who adopt such occupations must learn to cope with the small routine duties, even if mechanically.

Steve called to her, "Duncan is up!" All her thoughts and anxieties were with the remaining two, even though she wished no harm to Duncan.

Then Martin appeared, still holding the large underwater camera which Duncan helped him to unharness.

"Thank God!" murmured Rianna, unaware that she had spoken aloud. Then she realised that Holford had not yet come up.

"My air cylinder harness got caught in a projecting piece of timber," Martin was explaining to the others. "I was afraid to pull too hard – also I didn't want to damage the camera, but there I was, stuck fast like a barnacle."

Rianna's relief was immense, but there was still Holford to be accounted for. When at last his head appeared, she felt faint and gripped the taffrail with clenched hands.

Holford was evidently surprised to see her there and she moved towards him as he took off his mask.

"Thank you," she murmured, "for Martin."

She reached up to his face and kissed him, oblivious of his dripping wet suit, but only too thankful that both men had been spared.

Later, when all the team had changed into their ordinary dry clothes and had been medically examined by Steve, Rianna sat on deck under the awning and soon Holford joined her.

"Was it carelessness on Martin's part?" she asked.

He shook his head. "No. Something that could happen to

183

anyone, especially where there are wrecks. Timbers get pushed apart, broken in places. Actually, Martin has probably done some good work, for he managed to film a part of the wreck which we haven't been able to see before. So out of danger has come some good."

"I don't think I shall ever want to dive."

"Oh, but you must! How are you going to understand your husband's problems if you don't explore sometimes with him?"

She turned towards him, her face alight with mischief. "Oh, that's the first mention I've heard of a husband. So you do intend to marry me?"

"That was the idea in my mind," he returned with mock soberness.

"I think it's a good idea, but I shall have to consider it," she said demurely.

"You'll do all your considering this minute, my girl, or perhaps I shall tip you into the sea and see what happens."

"Ruthless, I see. All right, give me time and I'll practise diving – if it's only to please you."

"That's better." He bent his head to kiss the tip of her nose.

Yet it was only after daily swimming practice and then a check-up by Steve that Holford would allow Rianna to take her first dive with a snorkel, and then only, of course, in shallow water, and for no more than five minutes.

The other men in the team had told her of the wonders of the canals and tunnels and grottoes, the labyrinths that were full of jewel colours, but now for the first time she understood the fascination of this underwater world.

The island was full of volcanic vitality under the sea, the rock sides pitted with holes and passages. Fine pink weeds waved and sponges stretched out like hands.

She thought the sensation was like gliding about in liquid glass and now she felt secure, for Holford was at the other end of the six-feet "buddy line" and her end was wrapped about her palm, as he had shown her.

He motioned her to glance upwards and she saw what he

184

meant, for the sun shone through the water, turning it into the "ceiling of amber". She glanced downwards to find the "pavement of pearl", but as Holford told her afterwards, one cannot expect to find all the sea paved tidily with pearl slabs and today she could see only a green depth.

The pull on her hand reminded her that she must ascend with Holford and she was now surprised to discover how reluctant she was to leave this lovely dream-like world, silent and beautiful, yet challenging.

He came to the hotel that evening to have dinner with her and as she dressed, she remembered the amber glass ear-rings which she had put away, vowing never to wear them again unless she could be sure of Holford's love.

He noticed them at once. "So the pair are now restored to each other."

"What a fraud you were, pretending to throw one of them into the harbour!"

"I hope it was a lesson to you, not to tempt me to violence," he returned.

She had already shown him the colour photographs she had taken of the piece of coral he had given her. "Martin thinks one of these would make a good cover design for the book he's engaged on."

"Coral – amber – pearl," he murmured. "Jewels from the sea. I must find you a piece of real amber one day – and you can have it carved into a brooch of ear-rings. A string of pearls, if we can find the right kind of oysters – and you'll be set up."

"I might even find my own oysters, if I can dive well," she hazarded gaily.

"You might, and dazzle us all with your finds. You're not a bad pupil, but you've a lot to learn, though."

"About diving and the sea?"

"About most things – including me."

"Oh, I know that you're a complete enigma," she mocked. "It will take me a lifetime."

His intensely blue eyes danced at her across the table. "Two lifetimes. One for each of us – to learn with love."

To learn with love. It was a wonderful phrase, she reflected, and she would, indeed, be happy to spend her lifetime with this man as her loving and beloved tutor.

OMNIBUS— The **3** in **1** HARLEQUIN
only $1.75 per volume

Here is a great new exciting idea from Harlequin.
THREE GREAT ROMANCES — complete and
unabridged — BY THE SAME AUTHOR — in one
deluxe paperback volume — for the unbelievably
low price of only $1.75 per volume.

We have chosen some of the finest works of four
world-famous authors . . .

SARA SEALE

JANE ARBOR

ANNE WEALE

ESSIE SUMMERS ②

. . . and reprinted them in the 3 in 1 Omnibus.
Almost 600 pages of pure entertainment for just
$1.75 each. A TRULY "JUMBO" READ!

These four Harlequin Omnibus volumes are now
available. The following pages list the exciting
novels by each author.

Climb aboard the Harlequin Omnibus now! The
coupon below is provided for your convenience in
ordering.

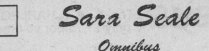

Sara Seale

Omnibus

Her natural talent for creating the very finest in romantic fiction has been acknowledged and enjoyed by a great many readers since very early in Miss Seale's career. Here, we have chosen three perfect examples of her best loved and most cherished stories.

. . . . CONTAINING:

QUEEN OF HEARTS . . . when Selina presented herself to her new employer at Barn Close, the exclusive country hotel in Coney Combe, Devonshire, Max Savant had one thought, to send this "child" on her way. Now, it was impossible for him to imagine himself, or his hotel being without her. But, he must, for he has just become engaged to Val Proctor . . . (#1324).

PENNY PLAIN . . . at Plovers Farm, near the village of Chode, in England, Miss Emma Clay is employed as assistant and companion to the rather spoilt young lady, Mariam Mills. Their relationship proves to be rather stormy, not the least cause of which is the country vet, in his country tweeds, the uncompromising Max Grainger . . . (#1197).

GREEN GIRL . . . Harriet listened to the incredible suggestion that she marry this total stranger and thus solve her dilemma, and the trouble which he himself was in. Whilst she knew full well that her own plight was quite hopeless, instinct warned her that Duff Lonnegan's trouble was far more serious than even he knew . . . (#1045).

$1.75 per volume

Jane Arbor
Omnibus

Jane Arbor chooses inspiring locations, peopled
with the most life-like characters, — then inter
weaves her gripping narratives. Her achievements
have brought her world renown as a distinguished
author of romantic fiction.

. . . . CONTAINING:

A GIRL NAMED SMITH . . . Mary Smith, a most
uninspiring name, a mouselike personality and a
decidedly unglamorous appearance. That was how
Mary saw herself. If this description had fitted, it
would have been a great pleasure to the scheming
Leonie Crispin, and could have avoided a great
deal of misunderstanding between Mary, Leonie
and the handsomely attractive Clive Derwent . . .
(#1000).

KINGFISHER TIDE . . . Rose Drake was about to
realize her most cherished dream — to return
to the small village of Maurinaire, France. To
manage her aunt's boutique shop produced grand
illusions for Rose, but from the very day of her
arrival, they were turned to dismay. The man
responsible was the town's chief landowner and
seigneur, a tyrant — living back in the days of
feudalism . . . (#950).

THE CYPRESS GARDEN . . . at the Villa Fontana
in the Albano Hills in Italy, the young, pretty
Alessandra Rhode is subjected to a cruel decep-
tion which creates enormous complications in her
life. The two handsome brothers who participate
come to pay dearly for their deceit — particularly,
the one who falls in love . . . (#1336).

$1.75 per volume

Anne Weale

Omnibus

The magic which is produced from the pen of this famous writer is quite unique. Her style of narrative and the authenticity of her stories afford her readers unlimited pleasure in each of her very fine novels.

. . . . CONTAINING:

THE SEA WAIF . . . it couldn't be, could it? Sara Winchester the beautiful and talented singer stood motionless gazing at the painting in the gallery window. As she tried to focus through her tears, her thoughts went racing back to her sixteenth birthday, almost six years ago, and the first time she set eyes on the sleek black-hulled sloop "Sea Wolf", and its owner, Jonathon "Joe" Logan . . . (#1123).

THE FEAST OF SARA . . . as Joceline read and re-read the almost desperate letter just received from cousin Camilla in France, pleading with Joceline to come and be with her, she sensed that something was terribly wrong. Immediately, she prepares to leave for France, filled with misgivings; afraid of learning the reason for her cousin's frantic plea . . . (#1007).

DOCTOR IN MALAYA . . . Andrea Fleming desperately wanted to accompany the film crew on the expedition, but Doctor James Ferguson adamantly refused stating that if she went along, he would refuse to guide them. But, Guy Ramsey had other ideas, and cunningly devised a scheme whereby Andrea would join them — in a manner which the Doctor could not oppose . . . (#914).

$1.75 per volume

Essie Summers ②

Omnibus

Without doubt, Miss Summers has become the first lady among those who write of the joy and splendour of romance. Her frequent use of locations in New Zealand, the country of her birth, has a timeless appeal to her readers throughout the world.

. . . . CONTAINING:

HIS SERENE MISS SMITH . . . she was very certain that never again, under any circumstances would she ever become involved with a member of the male management of any firm where she was employed. Then, William Durbridge came thundering into her life, and before long, was making his way straight to her heart . . . (#1093).

THE MASTER OF TAWHAI . . . Tawhai Hills Estate lay deep in the green rolling country of South Canterbury, New Zealand. It was here that the wealthy young Rowena Fotheringham came to work in the hope of being accepted for herself — not her fortune. She could easily have been, had she not decided to deceive the very first man who had ever really cared for her, complicating both their lives . . . (#910).

A PLACE CALLED PARADISE . . . no one must ever know the truth, the reason why Annabel Lee had come to Paradise, an isolated plateau at the head of Lake Wakatipu in New Zealand. She did not know how deeply she would come to love a man called Gideon Darroch, nor how it would affect him — if he learned her secret . . . (#1156).

$1.75 per volume